NINJAS
WITH FEATHERS

THE SUPER-SPECIAL MISSION OF ANGELS

NINJAS
WITH FEATHERS

THE SUPER-SPECIAL MISSION OF ANGELS

Written by JD HORNBACHER

Based on the book Angel Armies by Tim Sheets

DESTINY IMAGE® PUBLISHERS, INC.
P.O. Box 310, Shippensburg, PA 17257-0310
"Promoting Inspired Lives."

This book and all other Destiny Image and Destiny Image Fiction books are available at Christian bookstores and distributors worldwide.

Cover design by: JD Hornbacher and Robynn Lang

For more information on foreign distributors, call 717-532-3040.

Reach us on the Internet: www.destinyimage.com.

ISBN 13 TP: 978-0-7684-5962-3

ISBN 13 eBook: 978-0-7684-5963-0

For Worldwide Distribution, Printed in the U.S.A.

1 2 3 4 5 6 7 8 / 25 24 23 22 21

CONTENTS

INTRODUCTION

There is coming now a generation of young warriors...called My "War Eagles."

They will not bow to the enemies of their God. They will not listen to the propaganda and insults of hell...They will wrap themselves to Me and I will fly with them.

They will bring deliverance to tortured captives. They will not surrender in fear though surrounded. Though odds may be against them; it will not rattle them. They will not give up though the facts look gruesome.

Tim Sheets, *Angel Armies*

Psalm 91:11-13 TPT

God sends angels with special orders to protect you wherever you go, defending you from all harm.

If you walk into a trap, they'll be there for you and keep you from stumbling.

You'll even walk unharmed among the fiercest powers of darkness, trampling every one of them beneath your feet!

Ten years ago, God began to take me on a fascinating journey that led to the publication of my book *Angel Armies.* I am honored to introduce *Ninjas with Feathers,* which is based on that book.

The message of how Angel Armies assist us is vital for every generation, and it is exciting to be a part of this book, which is targeting our children and the coming generation. JD Hornbacher has done an excellent job of blending spiritual truths into an understandable and relatable format and interweaving them into a humorous, heartfelt, and lively storyline.

Your child will discover relevant truths concerning the wearing of God's armor, His purpose for our lives, and how to overcome their fears, just to name a few. These truths will remain with them all of their lives.

We encourage you to utilize the discussion questions included at the end of each chapter to open up dialogue with your child. You may even want to provide a journal for them to use as they read and answer the questions.

It is my prayer that this book encourages, sheds light on, and instills hunger to know more about the reality of angels and how they assist our everyday lives.

And by the way, I think even adults will like it!

Tim Sheets

Chapter 1

HEAVENLY HOMEWORK

It wasn't the sudden kick to my shin that stung the most. Or landing knees first on the school pavement. What stung the most was when Talia took a picture of me laying on the ground and sent it in a group text to the whole class which said:

Talia:
Zoe the Perfect's not so high and mighty when she's laid out on the sidewalk lol

I waited until Talia had strutted around the corner of the school building before I got up and brushed the dust off my new War Eagles hoodie. I considered fixing my tangled hair, but there wasn't a hairbrush in existence that could comb out my dark brown mess. I sighed. This was getting worse. Last time I tried to talk to Talia behind the school, Talia had just hurt me with words. Whoever wrote that dumb poem about sticks and stones had clearly never had a childhood. Whether Talia mocked me for going to church or for coming from another country, I had to admit—her insults were always very creative. "Your boyfriend is Jesus" and "I didn't know diarrhea was a skin color" were just some of the more memorable ones.

I sighed and grabbed the few things that had spilled out of my backpack—my phone, a pack of chocolate mint gum, and a few Lego pieces that had busted off the little treehouse I was building. Grayzon always teased that eleven-year-olds shouldn't play with Legos anymore, but my brother was a grump, so what did he know?

As I walked into the classroom, I made the mistake of looking Talia in her bright green eyes, which to me looked like pools of radioactive acid. Talia brushed her dark red hair behind her ear, and I noticed she had a fancy new watch on her wrist. She loved watches (especially if they weren't her own, I remembered). We were just pulling out our English textbooks when Mrs. Koopmans, our sixth-grade English teacher, announced our next big assignment. "We have wrapped up our unit on myths and legends. You have one week to write a report on a supernatural creature of your choice."

Aaliyah raised her hand. "Mrs. Koopmans? Can I do Bigfoot?"

"Why?" said Bennett from the other side of the classroom. "Because you think he really exists?" Some kids snickered. Aaliyah stuck her tongue out at Bennett. Those two made me laugh, which was why they were my best friends.

"You of all people should believe in Bigfoot, Bennett," Aaliyah said. "After all, he looks just like your dad."

The class burst out laughing. It took Mrs. Koopmans a few seconds to calm everyone down before she continued. "You can pick anything you want, whether it's considered real or fair-ytale."

"Fairy tales, huh?" Talia whispered to one of her friends, loud enough for me to hear. "I guess that means Zoe can pick God. Or his angels." They both giggled and made "cute eyes" at me while flapping their hands like little wings. I ignored them. Be nice, be nice, be nice, I told myself.

"You have until next Friday to write your report and hand it in," said Mrs. Koopmans.

The echoes of the final bell were still in my ears when Bennett bounced up beside me. Together we walked the crowded hall of Hamburger Middle School. "Friday! Friday! We're free! Another wonderful weekend to do whatever we want!" he sang, blue eyes twinkling behind chubby, pasty-colored cheeks.

"Oh please," said Aaliyah, knocking off Bennett's hat as she joined us, "you'll be doing the same thing you do every Saturday. Sorting your baseball cards. Me, I'm going shopping with my mom for a new outfit to wear to church on Sunday."

"Pink, of course." I said. Aaliyah always wore pink, not because she was super girly or anything, but because that bubblegum color went so well with her dark skin.

Aaliyah shoved me. "Earth to Zoe! Did you hear me?"

"Huh? What?"

"I asked what you're doing tomorrow," she said. Bennett fixed his hat and promptly shoved Aaliyah's backpack off her shoulder. Those two were ridiculous.

"I don't know. Dad's working, Mom has errands, and Grayzon just got the new Alien Exterminator game, so I doubt I'll see him leave his room. I'll probably just watch cartoons. It's not like I have anything better to do."

Laughter exploded from a group of my classmates standing by the front doors. They were pointing to their phones. I frowned, knowing what they were looking at. Something small buzzed past my ear, and I swatted it away. I stared at the ground as I passed by the kids, but I could feel their eyes on me. My steps fumbled as I suddenly felt another set of eyes watching me. But this felt different, more intimidating, more urgent. I whipped my head toward the dark corner by the water fountain.

No one was there.

Weird. I was sure I felt someone watching me. Bennett flung open the big front doors of the school and we were all blinded by the sun as we stepped out into the warm breeze. "Man! Summer is the best!" declared Bennett.

"No way," said Aaliyah. "I'm more of a winter girl."

"Well that makes sense," teased Bennett. "If my dad is Bigfoot, yours must be the Abominable Snowman."

I laughed and walked away toward the bike rack. "Have a good weekend!" I yelled to them. "I'll see you guys at church on Sunday!" Bennett and Aaliyah waved goodbye and continued teasing each other, but I was already lost in thought.

I hopped off my bike and entered the path that led through the forest of trees between the main road and my house. My phone dinged at me from my pocket, and I swiped through my phone to my message app, not even looking where I was walking. I could trot this path to my front yard with my eyes closed. Well, maybe not. I tried that once and smacked my head really hard on a branch, adding another scar to my collection of head wounds. Mom kept saying my head was magnetically attracted to hard objects. I read the message.

> Skeeter999:
> Can't believe Talia did that to you. What a tool. H8t her so much.

A tiny wave of anger washed over my thoughts. At least someone understood the frustration I was going through. I swatted at a circling mosquito and noticed I was passing through the small clearing on the path where my old playhouse still stood, covered in cobwebs and vines. I hadn't used it since...I shook my head free from the memory and tapped out a response.

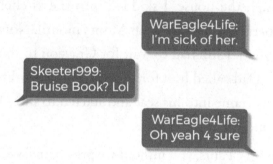

WarEagle4Life:
I'm sick of her.

Skeeter999:
Bruise Book? Lol

WarEagle4Life:
Oh yeah 4 sure

I emerged from the woods into my front yard without head-butting any trees, so that was a win. The second I opened my front door, I was blasted by the muffled sound of gunfire. I rolled my eyes. Grayzon must have run all the way home from his high school, which wasn't easy for him with his limp. I was sitting at the kitchen table having a snack when Dad walked in the door.

"Hey, kiddo. Want to see something cool?"

"Let me guess. Another trick shot video?"

He grinned. Dad was an awesome basketball player, and every day on his lunch break he would go to the basketball court behind the warehouse and film sweet trick shots. He pulled out his phone and showed me his latest one, where he bounced the basketball off of a garbage can and the chain-link fence into the net. He was super good.

"Whoa! That was amazing! Send it to me, I'll put it on YouTube for you."

Dad sent me the video and went into the kitchen to help make supper. An hour later, my mouth was watering as delicious smells wafted through the house. I skidded into the kitchen before the words "Suppertime!" had fully left Mom's mouth. Not that rushing did me any good. I still had to wait for Grayzon to shuffle into the kitchen after Dad called him for the third time. My brother finally slid his skinny frame into his seat and started to shovel a forkful of rice into his mouth.

"Hey, Hungry Pants, you mind if we pray first?" said Dad. Grayzon grumbled something but put down his fork. What was Grayzon

thinking? Like most Filipino families, we all knew that suppertime was super important, because food brings a family together, and family is everything.

"Son, would you like to pray?" asked Mom. Grayzon shook his head, which made me frown. He used to want to pray all the time. Dad finally prayed and we ate.

"How was school?" Dad asked as I started to devour my chicken.

Awful, I thought. "Great," I said.

Dad raised an eyebrow and stared at me for a moment. Shoot. He could always see right through me. "I know grade six is a tough time, Zoe. Lots of things are changing. I went through the same things when I was eleven."

I doubt it, I thought. "I know," I said.

"There's a lot of thoughts that can bounce around in that head, kiddo," Dad said, tapping me on the forehead. I hated when he did that. "Just remember that you can capture every thought—"

"And make it obey Christ," I finished. "I know, Dad. Sheesh." Dad raised an eyebrow at me, questioningly. "I mean...thanks. Sorry."

Mom turned to Grayzon. "What about you, son? How was your day?"

Grayzon gave a polite smile. "Grade nine, Mom. Homework, homework, homework."

"How are you going to have time to do any?" I said. "You're too busy playing video games." Grayzon glared at me, and I slunk into my chair. "What? It was just a joke."

I finished eating in silence.

After supper, I turned on the Chromebook in the living room and opened a new Word document. I didn't like leaving assignments to the last minute, or I'd be scrambling to get it done. I may as well write down a few thoughts now. I typed out a title.

ZOE'S REPORT ON _

I paused. What should I pick? Dragons? Centaurs? Ghosts? Centaur-ghosts? No, that wasn't a thing. I tapped my fingers on the keyboard, thinking. Then a thought popped into my brain. Maybe I should do what Talia and her friend were teasing me about. I grinned. Yeah, I'd show them.

ZOE'S REPORT ON ANGELS

My grin faded as I realized I had no idea what to type. What did I even know about angels? I knew that the Bible mentions angels a lot, and I believed those stories really happened, but I wasn't really sure that angels were still around today. I didn't know anyone who had seen one. Maybe they were just legends. Wow, this was going to be harder than I thought. Annoyed, I saved the document and closed the computer. I'd start tomorrow.

I did my chores, watched some funny YouTube videos with Dad, played a card game with Mom, and then finally collapsed into bed. I swatted at a mosquito buzzing past my desk lamp, and then noticed the open drawer containing a brown leather journal with a golden strap.

Written across the cover were the words Bruise Book (plus some scribbles where it used to say something else). I pulled out the book, flipped to a blank page, and thought about what I should write tonight. A wave of frustration ran through me. It was obvious what I should write about—the same thing I wrote every night. I reached for a pen.

Ribbit.

I peered over the top of the Bruise Book, where a tiny blue-green frog was staring at me. "Puddles, you little escape artist! How do you keep getting out of your tank?" Puddles hopped onto my lap and flicked her long tongue at the mosquito, but missed. I gave her a quick pat on the head and started writing.

I am so sick of Talia. Today she tripped me and sent a picture of it to everyone in class. It was so embarrassing! I try to be kind to her, but it never helps. I wish she would move or go to a different school. I can't imagine 6 more years with her! She's the worst!

That's why I called this journal my Bruise Book—it was the one place I could dump out all my hurt feelings, like bruises on my heart. My mind felt fuzzy. As I rubbed my head, I noticed something out of the corner of my eye. The picture on my dresser—did it just move? I frowned and stared at it. It was a picture of me, Bennett, and Aaliyah playing a stage game in Kids Church. The memory made me smile. I took a breath and looked back at my Bruise Book. I had filled a lot of pages in the last two years, which contained a lot of different emotions.

Pray about it.

The thought bumped to the front of my mind, as if someone had whispered it into existence. Where did that come from? I shrugged and put my pen to the page.

God, I hate these awful feelings inside of me. I don't know what to do with them all. And I don't know what to do about Talia. I want to trust that You are with me, but sometimes it's hard to believe that. I can't do this alone. Please send help.

Confident that I had poured out every drop of today's anger from my heart to the paper, I tossed the book back in the drawer, buried my head in my pillow, and closed my eyes.

DISCUSSION QUESTIONS

Zoe keeps a sort of diary—a journal where she writes down her hurt feelings. Do you keep a journal or diary? Do you write down hurtful things that happened to you or do you write down happier events?

Zoe's friends, Bennett and Aaliyah, are Christians and attend the same church as Zoe. It doesn't appear that Talia teases or bullies them. Can you think of any reasons that Talia targets just Zoe?

When Zoe wrote to God that she doesn't know what to do about Talia, she ended her entry with, "Please send help." Do you think Zoe meant for God to send an actual person? What ways, other than sending a person, could God help Zoe with her problem?

Chapter 2

THE GIANT IN THE KITCHEN

I woke up in a panic, drenched in sweat. I'd had the same dream six nights in a row: an odd-shaped creature with something slimy in its hand. It took me a full minute for my heart to stop racing. I glanced at my alarm clock.

8:12 AM.

Oh, come on! It was Saturday, my one day to sleep in! I wrinkled my forehead in frustration. I was never going to fall back asleep now. "Guess I'll get something to eat," I mumbled, crawling out of bed and sliding into my War Eagles hoodie. Suddenly, I froze. There was that feeling again, just like yesterday in the school hallway. Like someone was in the room with me. I gulped nervously and debated whether I should run away or karate kick the intruder in the face.

Obviously, I chose the karate kick.

I thrust my foot out behind me as hard as I could and screamed "Hi-yah!" knocking all my homework books off my desk chair.

They landed on a Lego castle set I had made, resulting in a plastic rainbow explosion. Aw, boogers! That took me like four hours to build! I smacked my hands to my face. Well, at least there was no intruder in my room. But I still felt jittery. These dreams were happening more and more often. And every time I woke up, I felt certain something was in the room with me. Not the creepy creature from my dreams, but something more powerful, more dangerous. The thought made me shiver, but for some reason it didn't scare me. It was almost like it was a good kind of dangerous (if that was even a thing).

I sighed. Only sugar could make my day better now. I made my way to the kitchen and grabbed one of the two identical boxes of Fruitee-Os on the counter. Mom had a weird habit of always buying two of everything. It was quiet in the house. Dad was already at work, Mom was probably out for her morning jog, and Grayzon had been blowing up alien invaders most of the night so he wouldn't be conscious until the early afternoon.

Crunch. Crunch. Crunch.

As I felt the sugar begin to hit my system, I lazily scanned my surroundings. On the counter by the stove sat my science project, with my "second place" ribbon attached to it. I had worked hard on that volcano. I would have gotten first place for sure if Karissa hadn't done such an awesome job on her huge model bridge made out of popsicle sticks. She was super smart. I wish I had the courage to tell her that. I took another bite and let my eyes drift from the volcano to other things in the room. The stack of cards from the game I played with Mom last night. My Unicorn Party cup that I just couldn't get rid of. The picture on the fridge of our foster child Kellia. The giant orange armored guy standing beside the fridge. Wait, what?

"Don't freak out," said the giant.

I immediately freaked out. Fruitee-Os erupted from my mouth as I fell off my chair and banged my head. I lay on the cold kitchen floor, gasping for breath. The massive giant stepped toward me, its huge hand reaching for me. I closed my eyes in terror and held my breath as its grip tightened around my arm...

And suddenly, I was being placed gently back in my chair. I dared to open my eyes and saw the giant just standing there, looking at me. It was massive, at least nine feet tall. Its head, which almost

touched the kitchen ceiling, was covered in a shining golden helmet which matched the rest of the armor on its muscled body. It kind of looked like a man. A huge, orange man dressed in armor. With enormous feathered wings. What was happening to me? Was this a dream?

"I know what you're thinking," the armored man said softly. "No. This is not a dream."

"You're...you're real?" I stammered.

"Extremely. If I was all in your mind, your mouthful of cereal would have passed right through me instead of painting my armor."

I glanced at his stomach, where the contents of my mouth were now sliding down his armor. "Oh. Right. Sorry about that."

"No, that was my fault. I probably should have waited for you to swallow before I exploded into existence."

I took a deep breath. Okay, if this was really happening, I was going to be brave. After all, didn't the giant tell me not to be afraid? He was smiling, and it didn't look like he wanted to eat me or steal my kidneys or take over the planet, so that was good. "Who..." I cleared my throat. "Who are you?"

"My name is Jophiel."

Jophiel smiled, which made my heart beat faster for some reason. I looked at his armor, the huge sword strapped to his back, and his massive feathered wings that filled half the kitchen. No way. Could he be...

"Are you an angel?!?!" I blurted out.

Jophiel's face split into a gigantic grin, revealing perfectly white teeth. His narrow eyes sparkled with...what was that? Delight? Wonder? Mischief? "Yes, I'm an angel," he said. I tried to say something profound, but no words came out. Jophiel crossed his arms and leaned against the fridge. "Take your time. It's a lot to process. I'm betting you have lots of questions."

A loud laugh burst from my mouth before I could stop myself. I blushed. "You could say that again."

"Good. That's one of the things I love about you, Zoe."

"You know my name?"

"Of course I do, silly. I've known you your whole life."

My mind felt like it was exploding. This was too much. How was this possible? Jophiel took a few steps and leaned down until he was almost face to face with me. I found myself involuntarily sliding back in my seat. His armor and skin almost seemed to be made of pure energy, and I wondered if I'd get a shock if I touched him. He breathed out softly, and I tried to recognize the smell of his breath. It was like...fresh cut grass and gummy bears and a rainy day in the mountains, all rolled into one. Jophiel raised his hand, stuck out his pointer finger, and gently touched my nose.

"Boop."

I decided in that moment that I liked Jophiel. A lot.

The armored angel stood up straight and, in one smooth motion, pulled the massive sword from his back and held it straight out in front of him. "Let me try this again. I am Jophiel, angel of the heavenly realms, protector of the earthly realm, and loyal servant of The Commander of Angel Armies." Jophiel lowered his sword slightly, glanced down at me, and winked. "But you can call me Joph."

My eyes were as big as dinner plates. "I have so many questions."

Joph chuckled. "Oh, I know. You ask more questions than any human I know. Patience, Little Warrior."

"But...if this is real, then...why are you here?"

"I need your help."

I snorted. "You need my help?"

"Uh huh."

"To do what, fluff your feathers? How could a little kid like me help you?"

"I need your help to accomplish my mission."

"What's your mission?" I asked.

"I'll get to that. But first things first." Joph looked down at the Fruitee-Os stuck to his armor. "Do you have a napkin?"

After Joph cleaned himself up, I convinced him to join me in the backyard. I didn't want Grayzon coming in and seeing me talk to a giant heavenly being. Wait, would Grayzon even see him? This was all very confusing. We stood in the middle of the yard, and Joph raised his hand and tossed my baseball casually into the air.

"Hey, wasn't that in my room?" I asked. "When did you grab that?"

"Right now," Joph said, catching the ball in his hand. "I'm very fast, like the wind."

I crossed my arms and smirked. "Prove it."

"You know that pink cowboy hat you won at the fair last year?" said Joph.

"Yeah. It's in my closet. Why?"

Joph's image flickered, almost like a video going out of focus for a second. He smiled and pointed to my head. I looked up and realized something was shading the morning sun from my eyes. I reached up and felt my cowboy hat. "Whoa! That was awesome!" I exclaimed. "Now this time, bring me something from Aaliyah's bedroom!"

Joph crossed his arms. "Excuse me, little miss, but you must have me confused with the Genie of the Lamp. I'm not here to grant you wishes or do tricks for you."

I blushed. "Sorry."

"I forgive you," Joph said and tossed me the baseball. We tossed it back and forth for a minute in silence, until I started giggling.

"What?" said Joph.

"I'm playing catch with an angel," I said, tossing the ball a little harder. "This is nice."

"It is, isn't it?" Joph replied. He caught my fastball with ease, and gently lobbed it back to me. "But Zoe, we really need to talk about what I mentioned earlier."

"Your mission."

"Well, yes and no. My mission has to do with your mission."

"I have a mission?" I asked.

"Everyone has a mission. Not just for your whole life, but even for right now. You were born at this time, in this place, around these people for a reason."

"Uh...are you sure?" I tossed the ball back. "I'm just a kid. What could I do?"

Joph was so shocked by my words that he missed the ball entirely. "Just a kid? Do you know what The Commander thinks about kids?"

My eyebrows crunched together. "The Commander? Do you mean God?"

"Yeah." Joph sighed dreamily. "He's the best."

"God has missions for kids?"

"Oh yeah. Important ones."

"But...why me? What makes me so special that I get a face-to-face meeting with an angel?"

"You asked The Commander for help." Joph put his hands on his hips and posed like a superhero. "So here I am." He picked up the ball again and tossed it at me. "So, you tell me—what do you need help with?"

I thought about what I had written in my Bruise Book last night. *I can't do this alone. Please send help.* I guess I did ask for this. But then I'd have to tell Joph about my Bruise Book. I shifted back and forth on my feet and tugged at my hair. "I don't know," I sighed. "I guess I just wanted God to like, stop everything bad that's happening."

"Whoa, that's a big request. Could you be more specific?"

"There's a girl in my class. Talia," I grumbled, throwing the ball as hard as I could.

"Ah," said Joph, understanding. "Yes, I am well aware of how you feel about her."

My heart skipped a beat. He knew? But surely he didn't know what I had been writing...

"So, what do you want me to do?" he said.

I thought for a moment. "Do you think you could come to school on Monday and fly her up to the top of the flagpole and give her a hanging wedgie?"

Joph made a tsk sound. "That is no way for a Daughter of the King to talk. And that's a hard no."

"Yeah, I didn't think so," I said. "But you've got to admit, it would be pretty funny."

Joph shook his head and threw the ball, right as I let out a big yawn. The ball knocked my cowboy hat off my head. That was close! Joph flinched. "Ooh, sorry. You okay, sleepyhead?"

"Yeah, I'm just tired," I said, picking up the ball. "I keep having this stupid nightmare, over and over." I whipped the ball at Joph and hit him right in the face. He didn't even blink. He just stood there like a statue, staring at me with concern.

"You've been having nightmares?" said Joph. "What kind of nightmares?"

I gulped. Thinking about them made me uncomfortable, like wearing pajamas made out of sandpaper. "I...well, there's this creepy little monster who's always whispering. And he's got something in his hands, and he keeps holding it out toward me." I shivered at the thought.

Joph frowned. "It's him."

"Him? Him who?"

Joph was lost in thought and didn't seem to hear me. He mumbled to himself. "What is your game, you little troublemaker?"

"Hey, I'm not a troublemaker!" I yelled, offended.

Joph looked over at me, remembering I was standing in front of him. "Huh? No, no. I wasn't talking about you. This is more serious than I thought. But it also explains a lot. Now we know what to look for..."

"What are you talking about?"

Joph walked over to my bike and picked it up. "Do you trust me?" he asked.

And I realized, in that moment, I did. "Yeah, I do, actually. I feel super safe around you."

"I get that a lot." Joph brought me my bike. "I am, after all, a holy being."

"That's cool," I said.

"So cool," he said. "Now look, I can't tell you everything yet. It's going to take some time to pull this off. But every day for the next week, I'll come to see you. We're going to go on a little...adventure."

"Um, Joph, I'm not sure I want adventure. I think I like things just the way they are."

Joph raised an eyebrow. "I know you don't believe that. And besides, what if this is about more than just you?"

I looked at the ground and kicked at the dirt.

"Look, I have an idea," said Joph. "You wanted help, right?"

I nodded. I just wasn't sure the help I was about to get was what I really wanted.

"Then we need to go get something," said Joph. "Come on, what else were you going to do today? Besides maybe fix your Lego castle. Sweet kick, by the way."

I blushed, remembering my attempt at a karate kick in my room this morning. "You saw that? Wait—was that presence I felt in my room...you?" Joph nodded, and a thought crossed my mind. "I thought I saw my picture move. Was that you too?"

"Just trying to get your mind off of negative things. You're getting better at noticing my presence." He handed me my bike and pointed toward the fence gate, leading toward the street. "Sooooo...?"

"I don't know..."

"What have you got to lose? If this is all a dream, then it will make for a fun story to tell Bennett and Aaliyah. If this is really happening, well...that will make a fun story to tell Bennett and Aaliyah, too."

"Not that they'd ever believe I was visited by an angel."

"You want to know why I'm here, and what angels are all about? There's only one way to find out. Now we can stand here and talk the whole time, or we can go." Joph turned and strolled toward the gate. "But I should probably warn you up front...if you come with me, you won't come back the same."

"You're being very mysterious," I said, gripping my handlebars tightly.

"That's kind of my thing." He opened the gate and looked at me. "Are we doing this, or not?"

I wiped a bead of sweat from my forehead and considered my options. Go on a mysterious journey with a giant angel warrior... or sit at home and watch boring cartoons. Right then, Mom jogged into the yard through the gate Joph was holding open. She didn't scream or fall or anything. Did that mean I was the only one who could see him?

"Hi sweetie. What are you doing?" she said, panting and stretching.

"Hi Mom. I was, uh...Would it be okay if I go for a bike ride?"

"As long as you wear your helmet. Where are you going?"

I glanced at Joph. "I'm not really sure. I guess...it will be an adventure."

"Okay, just be safe."

"I will," I said, hopping on my bike and following after Joph. "What could go wrong?"

If only I had known what was coming, maybe I wouldn't have said that.

DISCUSSION QUESTIONS

When you have a scary dream, what do you do? Do you know the verse about God not giving us a spirit of fear? You can find it in 2 Timothy 1:7. How do you think knowing that verse can help you to not be afraid?

The angel, Jophiel, told Zoe that he has known Zoe her whole life. If you knew you had an angel who really knew you, even knew your name, how do you think that would change how you think about things?

Joph tells Zoe that he's not a genie and that he's not here to grant her wishes or do tricks for her. Is that what you thought an angel was for? Before you started reading this book, what did you think an angel's duties were?

Do you believe God has a mission for you? What do you think it is?

What are some things you want God to help you with? Write them down in your journal.

Chapter 3

TWENTY QUESTIONS

We emerged from the path through the trees, having only hit my head twice—but it didn't really count since I was wearing a helmet. We started down the road that took us into town, me biking at a steady speed while Joph strolled casually beside me, somehow matching my pace. Angels made no sense. We traveled in silence for a few minutes until I couldn't take it anymore. "Let's play twenty questions," I said. I was a question person, and if he really was an angel, I had a lot of questions.

"Sure, I'll go first." Joph squeezed his eyes shut for a moment. "Okay, I've thought of something. It could be anything, even a puppy." Joph snorted and giggled. "Eeeee, I'm too excited to tell you! It was totally a puppy."

"No, not the game. I mean, I'm gonna grill you with twenty questions. I'm not supposed to talk to—or go on adventures with—strangers. And since you know me so well, it's only fair that I get to know you."

"Okay. Shoot."

I thought for a moment about what to ask a holy being from heaven. "Okay, have you really been with me all my life?"

"Uh huh."

"And you know all about me?"

"Uh huh. The Commander has a whole book written about you. I've read it."

"Okay, smarty pants, who's my best friend?"

"It's been a tie between Bennett and Aaliyah since you met them both last year."

"Pfft, that's easy," I said, struggling to think of more questions. "Okay, what do I want to be when I grow up?"

"A doctor."

"What will I actually become?"

"Uh uh uh, no cheating. You'll find out as you follow The Commander's path for your life."

"Well you can't blame a girl for trying."

"That was five questions already. Just FYI."

Sheesh, five questions and I hadn't even learned anything about him yet. "How old are you?" I asked.

"Pretty old."

"Like, as ancient as my dad? He's forty."

"Ha! I'm gonna tell him you called him ancient."

"Don't you dare!" I pointed at him, and my bike wobbled. I grabbed the steering wheel again before I crashed. Joph just chuckled.

"Next question," he said.

I looked at him in wonder. What to ask this big, orange, armored...oh. Never mind. "Why are you orange?" I asked.

"What color should I be?"

"Uh...I don't know."

"Well technically, my skin is a color that doesn't exist on earth and if you saw it with your eyes, your brain would melt. Orange is the closest I could come up with. We appear in lots of different ways."

My eyes went wide. "I like orange. Orange is good. Okay, why do you have armor?"

"That's what you wear when you're in The Commander's Army."

"God has an army?"

"Of course. That's how He fights battles."

"What battles?"

Jophiel puffed his chest dramatically. "The battle...for your soul."

I stared at Joph for a moment, and then did the "mind blown" expression with my hands, which again made me wobble on my bike. Joph just laughed at me. I didn't realize angels laughed so much.

"What did you think we did?" Joph asked.

"I don't know," I admitted. "Like, sit on clouds and play harps all day."

Joph rolled his eyes dramatically. "Well, I do play a mean harp, but no. We are defending you, secretly and unseen, fighting against evil forces."

I scrunched my nose in confusion. "When? How? I never see any of that happen!"

"I know." Joph struck a karate pose. "We're like ninjas. With feathers."

It was only a short ride from our house just outside town to the newly developed area that had a bunch of cool stores I loved. We stopped at the first intersection and waited for the green light. I fidgeted with my pedal as I waited impatiently. This light always took forever.

"Just wait," said Joph. The opposite light turned yellow, and cars started to slow down. I got back on my bike and positioned myself to rocket forward again.

"Just wait," Joph said again, putting his hand on my shoulder.

I frowned at him. "I'm just getting ready."

The other light turned red, and our light turned green as the walk signal lit up. I started to push off onto the road, but Joph roared, "JUST WAIT!!!!" It scared me so much that I fell off my bike and banged my head. I was just about to yell at Joph when a pickup truck blasted through the red light, past the exact patch of road I was about to ride onto. I sat there, too stunned to move. Joph picked up my bike and held it out to me. I shakily got to my feet.

"I said," Joph whispered, "'Just wait.'"

I got back on my bike, looked both ways about three times, and hesitantly biked across the intersection as the signal changed from "walk" to "don't walk." We continued down the block, Joph whistling softly beside me, until I finally spoke up.

"You...you just saved my life."

"Yep."

"And you're acting like it's no big deal."

"Well, it's not the first time."

I just stared at him. "What do you mean?"

Joph bounced into the air, flipped over onto his back, and floated lazily beside me, wings flapping softly in rhythm with my pedaling. "Do you have any idea how many times I've stopped you from being hit by a vehicle? Forty-seven." My mouth dropped open, and Joph continued. "Not to mention all the close calls with the swimming pool, the stove, the stairs, the—"

"Whoa, whoa, whoa," I interrupted. "You stopped those things from happening? But...Logan from church got hit by a car, and now he can't walk. Were there angels there?"

"Yes, of course."

"But they didn't stop it."

Joph looked up at the sky, still floating in place beside me. "The Commander's army doesn't stop every bad thing from happening, Zoe. We can't." Joph sighed, as if this was painful for him to talk about. "I know this is hard to understand. The Commander never promised you wouldn't get hurt, or sick. But He did promise that He would be with you, no matter what. That's where angels come in. We get involved, we warn, we get your attention."

"Like you just did with me."

"Exactly. We are always trying to help, but we can't control you, and we can't control other people. God gave you free will, which means you are free to make your own choices."

"But Logan didn't choose to get hit by a car!" I protested, wobbling on my bike again.

Joph lowered his head and tears formed in his eyes, which caught me by surprise. "But the driver of that car chose to ignore the warnings of his angel. And many of the terrible things people do to other people happen because they chose to ignore The Commander's wisdom and direction."

"It's not fair."

"That's the price The Commander paid to let His children have freedom. It meant that people are free to make their own choices—even bad ones." Joph wiped a tear away and looked at me with a fire in his eyes. "But The Commander never ignores the hurting or the brokenhearted. He was there with every person through every terrible time, protecting their hearts and giving them strength to keep going. Just wait until you get to watch the Movie of Your Life one day and see all the ways angels were protecting you. You have a Father who watches out for you. I promise."

I wasn't sure that was the answer I wanted, especially since I'd been thinking a lot about that lately. I didn't know what else to say though, so we rode in silence again for a while. When I looked over at Joph, he was pretending to ride an invisible bike beside me. I burst out laughing, and he just grinned.

"Joph..."

"Yes?"

"Thanks. For helping me. For always helping me."

"You're very welcome. It's both my honor and my duty."

"So...does that mean you're here to serve me?"

"No, I'm here to serve The Commander, who wants me to help you. There's a difference."

"Oh. Well for what it's worth, you're pretty awesome."

"Not as awesome as you."

"Pfft. Yeah right."

"I'm serious. In The Commander's eyes, you're more amazing than me, Little Warrior."

I stared at him in disbelief. "What are you talking about? I can't fly. I can't fight. I'm the size of your pinky toe. I don't even have a sword!"

"Are you sure about that?" Joph replied, a look of mischief in his eyes. I was going to ask him what he meant by that, but instead I smashed into a fire hydrant and flipped onto the grass by the sidewalk. I lay there and groaned, staring up at the clear blue sky until Joph's armored head appeared in my vision. "You probably should have been watching where you were biking. I feel like we just talked about this."

I groaned in pain. "Where were you on that one, big guy?"

"I feel like we just talked about that too." He pulled me to my feet (again) and handed me my bike (again). "You should consider wearing a helmet all day," he teased. "You only have one question left, by the way."

"What?" I exclaimed.

"Aaaaand that's twenty," Joph said matter-of-factly. I sighed, disappointed.

"Don't worry. We'll have lots more opportunities to—" Joph froze, looked upward as if listening to something in the sky, and frowned. "I've got to go for a minute. The Commander needs me. I'll meet you in front of Walmart."

And instead of disappearing, for whatever reason (probably because it looked super sweet), Joph flapped his wings hard and rocketed into the sky until he was a speck in the clouds.

Wow.

DISCUSSION QUESTIONS

Joph said angels were like ninjas with feathers. Do you like that description? How would you describe an angel?

Joph said he was always there in Zoe's life to protect her. Can you recall a time when you felt like you might have had help or protection from an angel?

Chapter 4

SHOPPING FOR SEEDS

It was 9:15 when I stopped my bike in front of Walmart. It was still early enough on a Saturday morning that the roads and parking lots were pretty bare, but they'd be full soon. I looked around for Joph. Huh. He said he'd meet me here. Maybe he was inside. Or maybe he was standing beside me, invisible. That thought made me glance over my shoulder nervously, but the only thing behind me was the rusty orange cat that always patrolled this street. Hm. Where was he?

Thump.

Joph landed hard beside me in a superhero-like crouch, his wings folding behind him. I screamed and toppled to the ground (because apparently that's what you do every time a heavenly being appears). Huffing on the pavement, I glared at him. "Can't you enter like a normal person?!"

Joph blinked. "But I'm not a normal person."

"I—okay, fair enough." I climbed to my feet, dusted myself off, and hesitated for a moment, considering something. Joph stared at me curiously as I walked over and poked his arm. He raised an eyebrow and I shrugged.

"Just making sure. It's still hard to believe this is real. You're...not exactly Cupid."

Joph gagged and rolled his eyes. "Ugh, please. You really think The Commander's angel armies are going be made up of chubby diaper babies with little bows and arrows? Give me a break. Come on, let's go."

I locked my bike up to the bike rack and started walking toward Walmart. It took me a few seconds to realize Joph wasn't following. I turned around and waved him over. "What are you doing? The entrance is this way."

"We're not going to Walmart," Joph said. "We're going in there."

I looked where he was pointing, and my heart skipped a beat. What? No way.

"The Dollar Store?" I squeaked.

"Yep. There's something in there we need to find," Joph replied.

"What is it?" I asked. "Can't we get it somewhere else?"

"Nope, we've got to go here. And you'll know what it is when you see it. Come on."

I took a step back and stared at the gigantic orange soldier with the ten-foot wingspan. "Ummmmm...you expect us to just waltz into that store...looking like that?"

"Trust me," said Joph.

"I do. It's actually kind of weird how easy it is to trust you," I said.

"Not really." Joph shrugged. "You know how sometimes kids at school say one thing, but then do something else?"

"Yeah. They lie, or they make promises they don't keep. I do it too, sometimes. Say things I shouldn't say, or..." I glanced at the Dollar Store entrance as we approached, "do things I shouldn't do."

"I know," said Joph. "But do you want to know something that will make you feel better? The Commander always tells the truth. He can't lie. He's only good. And when I come to talk to you, I'm saying only the things The Commander wants you to know. Which means everything I tell you is true."

Huh. That explained why it felt so easy to trust him. "Ugh, you're lucky. I wish I could know what's true all the time."

"You do? Well then, I may have just the thing..." Joph held up his hand. In it was a small golden belt. My eyes sparkled as I inspected it. It was so shiny. Like, Aaliyah's-lips-after-her-fourth-coat-of-lipgloss shiny. Joph held it out and I instinctively reached for it, like everything inside me was begging me to take it. It was surprisingly light for something that was clearly made out of gold.

"This," Joph said, "is the Belt of Truth."

"Wait, you mean the same Belt of Truth that's in the Bible?" I said, putting it around my waist. Joph nodded. "I remember reading about it in Ephesians—it's part of the Armor of God! But...why does armor have a belt?"

"Truth holds everything together. When you are connected to Truth that comes from The Commander, you'll be able to see things as they really are."

"Wow, this is super cool. The Belt of Truth..." I said, swinging my hips and modelling the belt in the middle of the parking lot. "I just never thought I'd get to wear a real actual belt."

"Most people don't," Joph replied. "But I figured since you get to see me in person, you may as well see the armor. Anyone who trusts in The Commander can put on their armor, even if they can't see it."

This was so cool. It looked pretty good on me, too! And just wearing it made me feel taller, more powerful. Together, we walked in the front doors. For some reason I expected alarm bells to sound, as if they had some kind of "angel warning system." But no sounds. Nobody even glanced our way. Oookayyyy...

Like every dollar store, this one was filled to the brim with random items—picture frames, coloring books, toilet plungers, puppy chew toys, and much, much more. I held back a slight smile. I could spend hours here. So much cool stuff! But then I remembered...I didn't want to be here. Not this particular store, anyway. We walked in silence for a couple minutes, strolling down random aisles. I kept looking back at Joph questioningly, but he would just smile and nod with his chin, encouraging me forward. After the fifth aisle, I noticed he was softly humming a tune that I recognized.

"Are you humming 'Wrap Myself in God and Fly'?" I said in astonishment.

"Uh huh. It's been stuck in my head all week."

"You listen to War Eagles? They're the greatest band of all time!" I tugged proudly on my War Eagles hoodie. "I have all their albums! Dad said I could even go to their concert this year if they come to town!" I paused. "Huh. Who knew angels had such good taste in music?"

Joph grinned and gave me a playful nudge. "Are we gonna stand here talking music all day, or what? We've got things to do."

My smile faded. Oh. Right. Things to do. "So, are you going to tell me what we're doing? I, uh, don't exactly love being here. It's been a while since..."

"Since what?"

"I'd rather not say." I turned and kept walking, wondering if he knew what I was going to say. Could angels read minds? I didn't think so...but to be fair, I didn't know that much about them. This whole experience so far was very...eye-opening. I was halfway down the cosmetics aisle before I realized where we were. I began to sweat.

"You okay, Tiny Champion?" Joph asked. "You look nervous."

My steps grew slower and slower. Eventually, I stopped, staring at an assortment of bracelets. My breathing became more rapid. Joph stopped beside me and put his hand on my shoulder. "So, you've been with me my whole life, right?" I asked without looking at Joph. "You've seen every decision I've made. The good ones, and the bad."

"I have. And I was with you the last time you were at this store."

"You were?"

He posed, karate style. "Ninja, remember?"

I swallowed, which was hard because my throat felt like a desert. "I haven't been able to come back here. I've been too scared."

"Well, we're here now. We needed to be here. Look closer."

I peered at the random collection of bracelets. I saw a very familiar bracelet, a shiny purple bracelet with green flowers on one half. Wait. What was that behind it? It looked like...I reached in and pulled out something the size of a football. It was dark and slimy and had weird veins all over it, which made it look like something out of a creepy alien movie. I stared at it. "It looks like...a seed."

"It is, in a way," Joph responded. "Do you notice anything strange about it?"

"You mean other than the fact that it's hiding in a dollar store?" Wait, I did notice something. But not from the seed. From me. My breathing was getting faster. A bead of sweat trickled down the side of my face. My heartbeat felt like it was doing a drum solo. What was happening? My head felt cloudy. Were people looking at me? Was this all a clever ruse by an imaginary feathered soldier to get me arrested for my terrible crime? I'm going to jail! Everyone's going to hate me! I'm a terrible person!

I gasped, threw the seed back onto the rack, and stood there shaking. I felt like someone had thrown me in a tub of liquid fear. All the color drained from my face as an elderly lady rattled her cart past me. "Are you okay, dear?" she asked in a wobbly voice. "You look a little peaked."

I had no idea what that word meant, because I didn't speak Old People Language, but I shook my head and pointed toward the seed, laying sideways on the rack. "I...just found something strange."

The woman looked where I was pointing, then frowned. "Hm, yes, very strange. I don't understand young people and their fascination with strange color combinations. Those bracelets are simply ghastly."

I tried to figure out what that word meant as she continued rattling down the aisle. Confused, I turned to Joph, still standing right beside me. "So...she couldn't see it?" I asked. Joph shook his head. "Wait, she couldn't see you either!"

"Oh, she could see me. Just not the same way you do." He smirked. "It's all part of my charm."

I looked at the seed again. It sure felt real. But why was I the only one who could see it? And what was it?

"It's a fear seed," Joph said, as if reading my thoughts. "They start small but grow over time, until they sprout. Believe me, you don't want to see what happens when a fear seed sprouts."

I looked at the seed again and unconsciously took a step backward. That thing just kept getting creepier and creepier.

Joph's voice was quiet. "This seed appeared the last time you were here."

I gulped. "You mean the day I stole the bracelet."

Six Months Ago

Mom and I had been here, looking for things to put in Puddles' tank, when I had seen the most beautiful bracelet. Shiny purple, green flowers on one half...I had to have it. But we only had enough money for frog supplies. My neighbor Regan had once told me that she'd taken a chocolate bar from here once on a dare, and nobody had even noticed. I had stood there for what felt like hours, shuffling back and forth on my feet, clenching and unclenching my sweaty hands. It was just a bracelet, and there were like thirty of them—surely they wouldn't miss just one. I could always come back and pay if I really needed to...

I had looked around to make sure no one was watching before grabbing the bracelet and stuffing it in my pocket. Mom was waiting for me at the counter to pay for Puddles' supplies. The cashier had looked at me and smiled, which I was sure was code for "I'm on to you and I've already called the cops. Enjoy life in prison!" But she just told us to have a nice day.

Regan told me nothing would happen. She was right, and she was wrong. I walked out of the store with a brand-new bracelet in my pocket...but I also had a heart thickly smothered in guilt.

I shook my head to clear away the memories and looked at Joph. "I made a really bad choice. And I've regretted it ever since."

Joph smiled sympathetically. "I know, Tenderheart. That's why this seed is here. It's been growing, feeding off your regret and worry about what you did and what kind of person you are. It's pure, concentrated fear. And the fear waves it's giving off are getting bigger and wilder." He shuffled his feet into a battle stance and reached to put his hand on the hilt of his sword. "Which means he's here."

I tensed. "Who's here?"

Someone cleared their throat behind me. "Excuse me, are you okay? You look upset."

I turned to see a teenage girl standing in the aisle. Joph growled. What was his problem?

"Oh, hi. Um, I'm okay."

"Crazy day, huh?" she said.

I frowned. "What do you mean?"

"I was just reading the news on my phone," she said, holding up a sparkly phone with the words "Trust No One" on the back. "Lots of weird stuff happening in our world. It makes me think that if I were your age, I'd just stay at home. I wouldn't be out here by myself, going on adventures."

"I'm not alone," I said, glancing at Joph.

The girl raised an eyebrow and looked around. "Really? I don't see anyone else with you."

Oh right. She couldn't see him. That was a stupid thing to say. I started thinking about all the stupid things I'd been saying lately. Maybe I shouldn't be here. Maybe I should leave, just go home and watch cartoons and forget about creepy seeds. The girl smiled at me, almost as if she knew something I didn't. I felt really confused but didn't know why. Joph placed his hand on my shoulder, and a sudden calm swept over me. "I...um...can I ask you a question?" I pointed at the shelf, not sure what else to do. "Do you see anything weird or slimy on that shelf? Like a prop from an alien movie?"

The girl looked where I was pointing and shook her head. "I don't see anything. But that's fine. Imagination is fun, right?" The girl leaned closer to me and whispered. "I'll let you in on a little secret. I still play make believe too. You know, talking to imaginary things like fairies. Or angels."

That got my attention. Angels? Joph wasn't imaginary...right? I mean, I was the only person who could see him. Just like an imaginary friend...Joph took a step forward and glared at the girl. "Back off. Now." The girl definitely flinched as if she had heard him. But she said she didn't see anyone...

I gave him a stink face and whispered, "What are you doing, Joph? That was mean."

"Zoe, are you still wearing your Belt of Truth?" said Joph. I looked down to double-check and nodded yes. "Then use it. You have been given the ability to see things as they really are, because of this gift from The Commander." When Joph said that name, the teenage girl flinched as if someone had slapped her. "Look at her using the Truth you've been given."

I looked at the girl again, and her image began to shift. "All right, you caught me," she said, her voice changing into something deep and scratchy. The girl jumped over my head and landed on top of the shelf—except she wasn't a girl anymore. I looked up and saw... well, I wasn't sure what I was looking at. Crouching on a pile of lava lamp boxes was the strangest, ugliest creature I'd ever seen.

DISCUSSION QUESTIONS

Joph refers to Zoe with different names for her, like Little Warrior, Tiny Champion, Daughter of God, Tenderheart, and others. What do you think about those names? Do you think those names describe Zoe? What do you think The Commander (God) thinks of you?

Zoe admits that she stole something. Do you think she still deserves to be called Tiny Champion or Daughter of God? Why or why not?

Can you think of a time when a fear seed would have started in your life?

Chapter 5

FEARMONGER

The creature was shorter than me, but wide and lumpy. Its purple-grey skin was covered in warts, and parts of it looked like it was melting. Its flimsy wings and long pointy nose were creepy, but the worst part was its eyes, which stared at me, full of hate, as a wicked grin split its face, revealing a scattering of sharp yellow teeth. "Peekaboo!"

I gasped and instinctively stepped behind Joph.

"Fearmonger," Joph growled, and the intense authority in his voice made me shudder. He drew his sword and took a step toward the little beast.

"Jophiel," Fearmonger replied. Although the creature puffed out its chest in defiance, I noticed that it had backed up slightly when Jophiel had stepped forward.

"I'm surprised you showed yourself, you little worm," said Joph.

"Ooh, you've been working on your insults, have you?" Fearmonger stretched his misshapen arms and bones cracked way louder than should be possible. "Why don't you leave that to the professionals, you clueless sack of muscled dog turds."

Oh, snap. I wonder what would happen if I called Talia that?

"What are you doing here? Why now?" Joph demanded.

Fearmonger winked at me. "Oh, I'm cooking up something special for little Zoe here."

"Leave her alone," Joph growled. Wow, he could be really intimidating when he wanted to be.

Again, Fearmonger flinched. "Threaten me all you want, feather-brain, but that one..." he pointed a curved knife of a finger at me, "is mine."

Joph roared and grabbed Fearmonger by the throat so fast I didn't even see him move.

Fearmonger choked and gasped, scrambling to get free. "Now, now," Fearmonger croaked. "Maybe we can come to some sort of an arrangement?"

Joph leaned in close and whispered so quietly I almost didn't hear him. "I will never work with you again. You had your chance, long ago." He held the tip of the sword up to Fearmonger's melty face. I expected the creature to scream or cry. But Fearmonger just relaxed and hung loosely in Joph's grip. "Put away your flashy toothpick, Jophiel," he said. "You know very well you can't do anything to me."

"Yet," Joph replied, grinding his perfect angel teeth together. Then he flung Fearmonger across the aisle toward a towering display of lotion bottles. Fearmonger flapped his little wings and caught himself in the air.

"You almost made me knock over this beautiful display," Fearmonger sneered at Joph. "Somebody worked hard on setting all this up." He turned to me. "This is just the start, little thief. You think Joph is helping you? His happy little stories are fairy tales. That Guy in the Sky doesn't care about you. He doesn't care about anyone. He'll just throw you away the second you do something that annoys Him. Trust me..." Fearmonger glared at Joph, "I know."

"Don't listen to him, Zoe," said Joph.

I was trying not to. But his voice and his words felt like they were buzzing into my brain.

"But me," Fearmonger continued, "I have all the answers you could ever need. Let's talk, you and I."

"I don't want to talk to you," I said, weakly.

"Oh, yes you do. You can't avoid me. You know me better than you think you do." The little monster pointed toward the fear seed and chuckled. "You see, I've got my roots in deep—and not just with you."

What did that mean?

Fearmonger smiled a wicked smile at me and leaned forward, but Joph stepped in front of me protectively. "Leave. Right now," growled Joph. Wow, he was really mad.

"Don't get your feathers all ruffled, Clouds-for-Brains. I'm going...for now." Fearmonger winked at me. "See you soon, Zoe."

 I didn't like the way he said that. Or the fact that he knew my name. He turned to leave, but then paused and turned back to the display of lotions. He kicked the bottom bottle out, and fifty bottles spilled across the aisle floor.

"Oops," Fearmonger said innocently. "Did I do that?" He laughed that awful, terrible laugh. And then he was gone.

I grabbed my tangled mane and covered my face in shock. "What. Was. That?"

"That," Joph said, "was Fearmonger."

"He was awful!" I declared, shaking off the shivers I still felt in my body. "I felt his voice trying to claw its way into my heart. When he was pretending to be that girl, what he said made me doubt myself."

"That is because he is a liar, a trickster, a demon sent to spread fear in the hearts of people."

I grabbed on to a shelf to support my shaky knees and gulped. "Demons are real too? I mean, I guess if angels are real, then it makes sense that demons are too..."

Joph grabbed my shoulder and peered into my eyes. I saw my reflection in his golden pupils, and a calm feeling swept through me. "Do not focus on him, Little Warrior. Do not let his lies get in your head. Be aware that he is up to something, but do not let your heart be troubled. The Commander is stronger, and He will help you fight Fearmonger and deal with the seeds he is planting."

Oh right. The seed. I wanted to keep talking about the lumpy little monster that just threatened my life, but I guess we'd have to come back to that. I looked back at the rack and found the seed nestled among the bracelets. What did it mean? What was I supposed to do with it?

"I don't like it. I want to get rid of it."

"Good," said Joph, as he bent down and started picking up the lotion bottles. "Because you're the only one who can."

"What, you can't hack it to bits with your sword?" I asked.

Joph shook his head. "It takes something special to get rid of a fear seed."

"Hm, let's see. I could grab a hammer from the tool aisle. But this is a dollar store, so I'm betting I'll crack the hammer before I crack the seed." I began to pace. "What else, what else...sledgehammer?

Jackhammer? Oh, I know! I could drop it in a big vat of acid! No, no, where am I gonna get acid on a Saturday morning..." As I pivoted in my pacing, I saw Joph standing there, holding up the same cheap bracelet I had stolen. My nose crinkled as I frowned in confusion. "What are you doing with that?"

"How much money do you have on you?"

I fished inside my pocket and pulled out the contents—a church invite card, an arm from a Ninja Turtle, some candy wrappers, and a bunch of change. I quickly counted. "Three dollars and ten cents."

Joph didn't say anything. I grew silent. The only sound was the rattle of the old lady's cart as she approached the counter to pay for her items.

Oh.

Oh no.

No no no.

I looked at Joph with wide eyes. "You mean..." Joph remained stubbornly silent. I adjusted my War Eagles hoodie and glanced at the lady at the counter, who looked like a cute little potato with an explosion of red hair. Oh man. It was the same cashier. No way. Everything in me pulled at me to run to the employee area and out the back exit, but for some reason I started walking forward. Stupid legs! Were they trying to get me arrested? But I kept walking until I was standing at the front counter.

"Hi sweetie," said Potato Lady. "How can I help you?"

"Um..." I shifted my feet nervously and looked down. The money in my hand felt like it weighed three hundred pounds. She waited a moment, then cleared her throat.

"Maybe I should ask your grandpa," she said.

Huh? Grandpa? I looked up at the cashier, whose nametag said Marge. She was looking beside me. I turned toward Joph, but he wasn't there. Standing in the angel's place was a skinny old man with a face like a raisin. The man winked at me from under his orange fedora hat.

"No," said Joph, in a voice that wasn't his own. "My...grand-daughter can handle it."

I was speechless until Marge cleared her throat. "Sweetie? Were you looking to pay for something?"

I snapped back to reality and turned. "Um, yes. I want to pay for a bracelet."

"Okay," said Marge. "Where is it?"

"Well, that's the thing." I spared a quick glance at Joph-now-Grandpa, then took a big breath. "I kind of...stole it...six months ago."

Marge leapt onto the counter, grabbed a megaphone, and shouted, "I KNEW IT! THIEF! THIEF! YOU'RE GOING TO JAIL, SUCKER!" At least, that's what I had expected Marge to do. Instead, Marge smiled compassionately. "Oh. I see."

"I'm really sorry," I said, as I tried to stop tears from forming in my eyes. "I'd like to pay for it now."

"Of course, honey. Stolen bracelets cost two dollars and a sincere apology. You've already apologized, so I guess that'll just be two dollars." Marge held out an open hand, and I quickly—maybe too quickly—dumped the change in her hand. I didn't know what else to say, so I just awkwardly turned to leave.

"Just one more thing," Marge said, and I cringed. I knew that was too easy. I slowly turned around to find Marge holding up a green lollipop. "Now that all is right in the world, it's important I give you something special. It's a Forgiveness-flavored sucker." Marge winked and glanced at the old man beside me. "If that's okay with your grandpa."

I looked at the warrior of light shoved into this skinny old body and stifled a laugh. Joph's voice had a melodic twang to it as he chuckled. "I think she's learned her lesson. That's fine with me."

I smiled and accepted the lollipop from Marge. As soon as we were back outside, I let out a huge breath that I didn't realize I had been holding. "Whew! I feel so much better! Thanks 'Grandpa.'"

But when I turned around, the big orange angel was back. "Who are you calling 'Grandpa'?"

"So you can disguise yourself as anyone?" I said, popping the sucker into my mouth. Green apple. Yum.

"Sure. We've been doing it since the very beginning of time. You never know when someone you meet might just be an angel in disguise."

A light went on in my head. "Ohhhh! That's why the old lady didn't freak out when she saw you."

Joph chuckled. "Actually, she slipped me her number on this piece of paper. I think granny has the hots for me."

"Ew!" I yelled, and then burst out laughing. "Wait, that doesn't make sense. Those people in the store saw you, but my mom didn't notice you at all! Were you invisible to her?"

"Yes." Joph just shrugged. "I pick and choose when I want to be seen and when I don't. It's fun."

I nodded, and then my eyes suddenly went wide. "The seed! We left the seed in there!"

Joph smiled and held out his hand. "You mean this seed?"

It was the same seed, but different. It was half the size it had been, and it seemed to still be shrinking. Joph placed it in my hand, and as I watched, bits of the slimy blue shell crumbled and fell off. I

watched in silence as the fear seed shrank and disintegrated, until there was nothing left but ash in my hand. "But..." I fumbled through my words. "Why did it do that?"

"You tell me, SmartyPants."

I searched my thoughts. The fear I felt when I held it. The worry it represented. The hold that fear had had on me for months, even though I had—for the most part—forgotten about the whole encounter. And then I watched myself approach that counter. "I faced my fear," I realized.

Joph winked. "You faced your fear."

I smiled, and together we walked toward the bike rack near the Walmart.

"Can I tell you something?" I said as I unlocked my bike.

"Sure."

"It felt really good to get that off my chest. I didn't know the truth would be so...freeing."

Joph leaned over and tapped my Belt of Truth. "It is a special privilege to wear the Belt of Truth," Joph said. "Truth is very, very important to The Commander. Everything He says, He does—that makes Him totally trustworthy. And you should be trustworthy, too. After all, you were made to reflect Him to this world."

"Wow, that's a lot of responsibility," I said, looking at the golden belt on my waist. "I'll do my best. So...where's the rest of the armor?"

"Be patient, Little Warrior. Every piece is yours to have. And you're going to need them, because that seed you held..." Joph paused, as if deciding if he should say more. "It's not the only one."

My mouth dropped. "You mean there's more of them? How? Where?"

"That's something we'll have to figure out together."

"You mean you'll lead me?"

"No." Joph tapped me on my chest, just above my heart. "He will lead you. I'm just here to make sure you get to where you need to go, and help you see it through."

"He will lead me? You mean...Holy Spirit?"

"Smart girl," said Joph. "I'll see you tomorrow at church. Don't forget your bike."

I grabbed my bike off the ground and opened my mouth to convince Joph to stay, but he was already gone. Like, "Batman-vanishing-off-the-rooftop" gone. Wow, I wish I could do that. I was discovering that angels were pretty amazing. In fact, I had already learned a lot about angels today. Hey, I should write down notes for my report as soon as I got home!

I shook my head in amazement. I thought everything I learned about angels would come from the Bible and the internet. I never imagined I'd be taught by a real live angel. I got on my bike and started pedaling home, feeling better than I had in a long time.

After all, I had a bracelet hidden in my bottom drawer that I could finally wear, guilt-free.

And that made me smile.

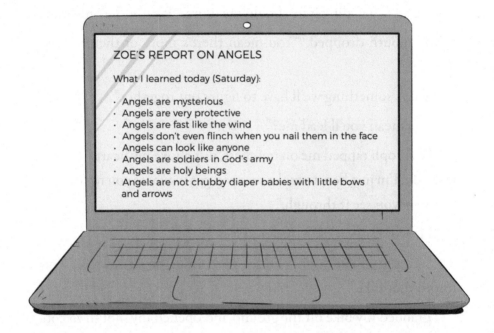

ZOE'S REPORT ON ANGELS

What I learned today (Saturday):

- Angels are mysterious
- Angels are very protective
- Angels are fast like the wind
- Angels don't even flinch when you nail them in the face
- Angels can look like anyone
- Angels are soldiers in God's army
- Angels are holy beings
- Angels are not chubby diaper babies with little bows and arrows

DISCUSSION QUESTIONS

Joph appeared as an old man in this chapter—an angel in disguise (Hebrews 13:2). Do you think you've ever seen anyone who might have been an angel?

When Zoe faced her fears, the slimy fear seed began to shrink. Do you have any fears that you need to face? Did the fear shrink or disappear after you faced it?

?

Chapter 6

DANCES AND DOUBTS

My alarm woke me right as the creepy creature from my dream reached out his hand to me. I now knew it was Fearmonger holding a fear seed, but it didn't make the dream any less scary. I shook my head and stretched. I was tired, but it was Sunday. That made waking up worth it. Church was my favorite part of my week. Just another reason the kids in my class thought I was a weirdo. But that's only because they've never been to church—or at least not to one that has great kids' programs.

I was shoveling Fruitee-Os into my mouth when Dad walked by and playfully tussled my hair. I smiled (even though a chunk of my hair got caught in his wedding ring and he had to yank his hand free). Last night I had told Mom and Dad about what I had done at the Dollar Store. They were really disappointed that I had stolen something, but when I told them I had told the truth and paid for it, I didn't even get grounded! I looked at my Belt of Truth, proudly displayed on my waist. Who knew truth could be so awesome? (Well, besides Joph—he seemed to know everything.)

"Get enough sleep last night, Grayzon?" Mom asked as we all piled into the car. Grayzon looked like a zombie. He mumbled a response, but that just made him sound like a zombie, too. I chuckled. Well, at least he got out of bed today. My smile faltered a little when I realized Grayzon had been doing this a lot lately. He seemed more reluctant to go to church. I was seeing less and less of him as he hid in his room, and whenever he came out, he seemed grumpy. Maybe I could cheer him up.

"Are you looking forward to church?" I asked him. He just made a grunting noise. "Wow, really? Sounds neat." Another grunt. "You don't say! And then what?"

This time, Grayzon turned and glared at me. "Zoe, why are you being so annoying?"

"I was just joking around. We used to joke around together all the time." My voice got quiet. "We used to have fun together."

"Yeah." Grayzon shifted in his seat and rubbed his leg. "I remember what having fun got me." He turned and looked out the window, ignoring me. Well, that didn't work.

Dad said goodbye to me when we got to the Kids Church section and headed off to set up pylons in the parking lot. I walked down the hall toward the middle school auditorium and saw Aaliyah, dressed in a cute pink top, heading my way. I yelled down the hall at Aaliyah. "Hey, A!"

"Hey Z!" said Aaliyah. "I told our teacher that I would get the supplies for the game. If you see Bennett, tell him he's supposed to be helping me. Do you want to start setting up chairs?"

"Sounds good," I said as she strolled away, leaving me alone in the empty hall. I turned around to head for the middle school auditorium, but Joph was standing in my way. I jumped so high I thought I was going to bang my head on the rafters. Joph burst out laughing. "Stop doing that!" I yelled, looking around to see if anyone was watching. But the hallway was empty.

Joph wiped a tear from his eye and sighed. "That never gets old. Nice bracelet, by the way." He pointed to the purple plastic bracelet on my wrist, which made me smile. Joph rubbed his hands together in anticipation. "Alright, let's do this. Today's going to be a good day."

"Why? It's just a normal Sunday."

Joph raised an eyebrow. "Oh, is it?"

"Isn't it?"

"I don't know, is it?"

"Can you stop doing that?"

"I don't know, can I?" Joph teased. I punched him in the arm, which hurt my hand because I accidentally hit his wrist guard.

"Ow! No fair, you have armor."

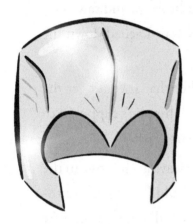 "Oh, speaking of which...time to get your head in the game." Joph chuckled and held up a golden metal helmet. "Get it? Your head? Because it's the Helmet of Salvation?"

I rolled my eyes. Joph sighed and handed me the helmet. My eyes sparkled as I stared at my reflection in the shiny metal. I crinkled my nose as I noticed my hair. Even though I tried to comb it for church, it was still a tangled mess. But then I realized nobody would notice once this bad boy was on my head! I grinned until another thought hit me. "So, these pieces of armor...I don't have to, like, earn them?"

"You can't earn something that's already been given as a gift, silly. Now come on, we should probably start searching."

"For what?" I said as I pulled the helmet down over my crazy hair.

"The next fear seed."

"At church?" I exclaimed. "How could there be a fear seed at church?"

"Oh, you'd be surprised," Joph replied. "Yes, this is The Commander's House and it's protected, but people are people and they still bring their doubts and fears with them when they walk in the doors."

With that, Joph walked away. I hurried down the hall after him. We passed a couple other kids carrying craft supplies, but if they saw a big orange angel beside me, they didn't say anything. We walked side by side for a while. At first, I was following Joph. But after a bit, I realized Joph had trailed back and was letting me take the lead. Okay. I could do this. Just find a seed. No big deal. It's just a disgusting object of awfulness planted by the grossest thing I'd ever seen. Even grosser than the time in art class when Chandler let a huge slimy booger hang from his nose and then snorted it back in. I gagged a little just thinking about it.

I walked into the middle school auditorium. Bright lights lit up the stage, decorated for this month's new theme. "Hi Zoe!" yelled Bennett. He was fiddling with the lighting controls, making the stage lights flash around like a lightsaber battle while he sang the Star Wars theme at the top of his lungs. I laughed. Bennett and I both loved being the first ones here—it made us feel important to help out, and we also got to goof around a little.

"Hey Bennett! Aren't you supposed to be helping Aaliyah with game supplies?"

"Whoops! Yep, I forgot!" said Bennett, who took off running out the door. "Sorry to leave you alone on chair duty!"

"It's okay!" I said, but he was already gone. I looked up at Joph and smiled. "I'm not alone."

"How can I help?" said Joph.

"Grab some chairs and start making rows."

Joph grabbed a stack of heavy chairs in each of his hands and walked to the front of the room. Wow! This was going to go super quick with muscles like that! I pointed to the front corner. "Start up there. That's where I usually sit. I, uh...like to be off to the side so people don't hear me when I worship," I admitted sheepishly.

Joph dropped his stack of chairs and clapped his hands together. "Oh, I love when you sing worship songs!"

I crinkled my nose. "Why? I have an awful voice."

"We're not listening to your voice. We're listening to your heart."

"We?" I asked.

"Yeah! When you worship, it's like...it's like when you turn on the porch light and all the moths swarm to it. Angels are drawn to praise. It's our favorite."

"Oh. So I have an angelic audience." I smiled awkwardly. "Great. No pressure..." Joph chuckled and started lining up chairs so fast it made my head spin. We worked in silence for a few minutes, until I couldn't hold it in anymore. "Why are you helping me?" I asked.

Joph glanced at me as he balanced a stack of chairs on his pinky finger. "Because you asked me to, silly."

"No, I mean..." I took a breath. "Why are you helping me with Fearmonger and the seeds and everything? I'm nobody special."

"Well first off, I'm helping you because that is what I was literally created to do. And second, you are very special. It seems like most kids these days think much too little about themselves. That's not what The Commander would say about you."

"What do you mean?"

Joph put down his stacks of chairs and slowly walked over to me. "You, oh Daughter of the King, are His greatest treasure. His greatest delight. His top priority. In His eyes, you are greater than the tallest mountain, the most beautiful sunset...greater than even His angels."

"Whoooooaaaa. Greater than you?" I said in disbelief. "Doesn't that make you jealous?"

Joph leaned down to look me in the eyes. "You're silly." He tapped my nose. "Boop."

As he walked back to his stacks of chairs, I thought about what Joph had said. "Sometimes I forget how much He loves me. I forget how He's changed me." I said, trying to pull off a stubborn chair stuck to the others.

"Do you remember the first time you said yes to Jesus?" Joph said, finishing another row of chairs. "Like, really really said it and meant it?"

A happy memory flooded my mind. "Yeah. I do. It was during my small group at church, like three years ago. We prayed the prayer we said every week, but something was different. There was this feeling in my stomach, like thirty rhinos tumbling around in a washing machine made out of Jell-O."

Joph snorted. "You certainly have a way with words."

"Thanks." I continued, "I just knew in that moment that God was real. That Jesus died and came back to life to give me new life. I felt loved and rescued and so alive. It felt...perfect." I sighed happily. "Like, 'pickles and maple syrup' perfect."

"Yes, it's a beautiful—wait," Joph wrinkled his nose and stuck out his tongue in disgust. "That's your definition of perfect?"

"Uh, yeah! Have you tried pickles and syrup?"

"No. Have you tried freshly squeezed rainbow? Now that's perfection."

I rolled my eyes at him and set out the last chair of the last row. "Anyway, the point is...it was a pretty great moment."

"I know. I was there, remember? Well, for most of it. I did take off right after."

I whipped around to look at him, but my crazy hair followed my head and smothered my face. I batted it out of the way. "You left? Why?"

"Because I had to let all my angel buddies know what just happened, so we could start the party!"

"You had a party for me?"

"Oh, girl! You have no idea. There ain't no party like an angelic party! We bounce around like puppies on a sugar rush every time someone makes Jesus the leader of their life."

Joph busted out a dance move I had never seen before. Every pop star dance choreographer in the world would have paid top dollar

to witness what I just did. All I could do was grin. I crossed my arms and leaned against the wall to watch. Then my butt started buzzing. Well, not my butt—rather, the phone in my back pocket. I pulled it out and checked the message.

Skeeter999:
Thanks for the invite to church, but I'm still in bed. Late night. Besides, church isn't really my thing. Pretty hard to believe a lot of that God stuff.

Attached was a meme of a cartoon God spanking the world and saying, "Gotta love me!" I don't know where she kept finding these memes. I didn't really like them, but they were kind of funny, I guess. As I put my phone back in my pocket and went

back to watching Joph (who was still dancing up a storm), I kicked something with my foot. It wobbled around to the front of me, and I looked down.

It was a fear seed.

I frowned and stared at it. Why was this here? In church? In the corner of the room, where we always...

Oh.

Suddenly I knew what it was and what it represented. My cheeks flushed in embarrassment. Joph paused mid-dance and stared at me.

"Zoe? Are you okay?" Joph hurried over to where I had slumped down to the floor beside the seed. He crouched beside me, patiently silent until I spoke.

"I know why this is here. Sometimes..." I couldn't find the words, but I knew I needed to say them. "Sometimes I doubt if God is good." I paused, cringing, expecting Joph to yell at me, or for a lightning bolt to hit me from heaven. But nothing happened. After a few anxious seconds, I continued. "A couple of months ago, we were in small group and one of the other kids said something that I couldn't get out of my head." My heart hurt just thinking about the memory. "The kid said, 'If God can stop bad things from happening, why doesn't He? Either He doesn't care, or He isn't real.' And that made me think of Talia, and how she bullies me every day. God could stop it. I know He could. And so, I just kept thinking...maybe He doesn't care, or maybe He's not real." Joph listened quietly. I took a big breath. "I remember thinking, 'What if this is all made up?'"

"Do I look made up?" said Joph, spreading his arms proudly.

"But that just proves my point! How do I know you're real? I don't know if any of this is really happening. Nobody sees angels!" Joph raised an eyebrow. I sighed. "Not anymore, anyway..."

"You'd be surprised how many people see us. Sometimes we need to show up in person. There's plenty of examples in the Bible: Abraham, Gideon, Mary, even Jesus! So yeah, we show up. But you'd be even more surprised by how often we get involved in your life without you even realizing it."

"But why? Why do you even care about us?"

"Because I care about what The Commander cares about. And there's nothing He cares more about than you."

"I hope that's true."

"It is, Little Warrior. And one day, you'll understand. The Commander is amazing. I get to stand beside His throne, watch how He acts, listen to how He talks and what He says. And His smile..." Joph sighed dreamily. "His smile feels like ten thousand happy moments high-fiving my heart at the same time." He clapped his hands together excitedly. "Oh, if you could see Him the way I see Him! If only you really knew Him like I do! But the best part is, one day..." Joph leaned in close to me and whispered, "you will. And I guarantee that when you truly encounter Him, you'll cheer and jump for joy."

Right then, there was nothing I wanted more. Then a wave of guilt washed over me. "I feel bad for doubting. I don't like having those icky thoughts," I said.

"The Commander isn't scared of your doubts. He's Lord of all, no matter what you think. Whether you believe in Him or not, He's real." Joph tapped me on the head and I heard a metallic clang. Oh right, I was still wearing the Helmet of Salvation. "When His Son died and rose again, He freed your mind and now guards your thoughts. Even your icky thoughts."

I stared at the fear seed on the floor in front of me. "The things Fearmonger said back at the store..." I nervously scratched the back of my hand. "Something inside me wanted to believe him, Joph. What he said made sense, in a weird way."

"That's what Fearmonger does best, Zoe. He divides people, whispering quietly. He speaks in half-truths. It's almost right. It's almost true. And without realizing it, people are left with seeds. Just like you."

I suddenly noticed something. "Huh. The seed is wet, and so is the spot where I kicked it," I said. "What do you think that means?"

"It means it's been freshly watered, to make sure it's growing."

I looked around nervously. "Does that mean Fearmonger is here, right now?"

"If he is, he's hiding. His kind don't like to be in places like this. The Commander's presence is so strong, they can't stand it." Joph looked around the auditorium and smiled proudly. "Lots of great stuff happens here. What a great reflection of Jesus. No wonder His Church is going to win!"

I nodded. Church was pretty great. "Okay, last question for today."

Joph rolled his eyes. "Yeah, right..."

I smacked him playfully. "I'm learning more every day about who God is and what He's like. But you...you get to be with Him all the time. What's that like?"

Joph sighed dreamily. "He's the best." He stared off, smiling.

I snapped my fingers. "Hey! Earth to angel!" Joph shook his head and looked at me.

"What?"

"What's it like being with God all the time?"

"It's kind of overwhelming to be honest. He makes me smile, but He also makes my knees shake."

"Your knees shake? You mean I should be scared of God?"

"No, silly. Never be scared of Him. He's the safest. But He is also so big and awesome and has all the power in the universe! When the Bible tells you to fear The Commander, it means respect Him, be amazed by His awesomeness. You can fear Him, yet still feel so safe."

"That doesn't make sense."

"Exactly," Joph said, and booped me on the nose.

I crossed my arms as he stood back up to his full height. "One of these times, I'm gonna boop you back."

"Pfffft, yeah right," Joph scoffed. "You're too short."

I grabbed the fear seed and got to my feet as Bennett and Aaliyah entered, carrying bins and boxes full of random game supplies. "Whoa, Z!" Aaliyah said in shock. "You already finished all the chairs by yourself? Do you have superpowers or something?"

"Something like that," I said, winking at Joph.

Bennett frowned at me. "What's up with you? You seem different today."

"What do you mean?"

"Like, more confident or something."

"I don't know. I guess...I guess I'm just tired of doubting myself. And God."

Aaliyah pulled a squishy ball out of a bin she was carrying and threw it at my head. "Look at you, capturing thoughts and making them obey Christ. Isn't that what your dad always says?"

I threw the ball back at her, which made her almost drop everything she was carrying. Dad was right. I glanced at the fear seed I was still holding in my hand and realized so many thoughts of fear and doubt had been trying to make a home in my mind. I gently touched my head and remembered I was wearing the Helmet of Salvation, which protected my mind. I needed to choose what thoughts I kicked out, and what kind of thoughts I wanted to stay.

"So if you're done with doubting," said Bennett, "what do you want to believe?"

I smiled at both of them. "I can't prove God is real. I can't even prove that God is good. But I choose to believe it, because God is bigger than my doubts. I know in my heart He's real and He's good, because He's done so many great things in my life, and He gave me awesome friends like you guys."

"Zoe's right, you know," Bennett said to Aaliyah.

"About what?" said Aaliyah.

"That we're awesome."

Aaliyah rolled her eyes and threw a ball at Bennett, who struggled to keep his supplies from spilling while he threw some supplies back at her. I was about to break up their battle when I felt the fear seed tremble in my hand. I lifted it up to my eyes and watched as it crumbled into ash in my hands. I laughed in victory, which made Bennett and Aaliyah stop throwing things and look at me again.

"Take that, Fearmonger," I quietly threatened. "Wherever you are, I'm coming for you and all your stupid fear seeds."

"Yeah girl!" Aaliyah grinned. "I have no idea what you're talking about, but I like your feistiness!"

Bennett crinkled his nose. "Fearmonger? Is that a new band? I've never heard of them."

I just laughed and fist-bumped both of my best friends. They cleaned up their game supplies and walked toward the stage. Joph stood beside me and smiled at them. "See? You've got more than just angels watching your back, Zoe. You need good friends—like those two—to help you in life."

"People should be arriving soon." Bennett yelled at me from the stage. "I don't know about you guys, but I'm ready for a good morning with God!"

"Yeah," Joph sighed dreamily beside me. "He's the best."

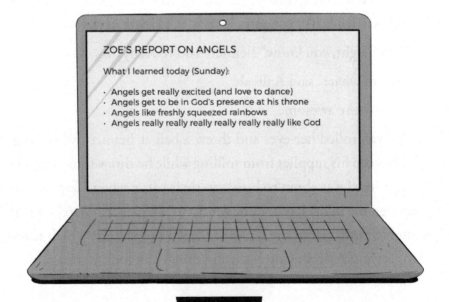

ZOE'S REPORT ON ANGELS

What I learned today (Sunday):

- Angels get really excited (and love to dance)
- Angels get to be in God's presence at his throne
- Angels like freshly squeezed rainbows
- Angels really really really really really really like God

DISCUSSION QUESTIONS

Zoe was surprised that there could be a fear seed somewhere in her church. Does it surprise you that people bring their doubts and fears into church? What else do you think people might carry with them into church? Can you think of a better place to bring those things?

Joph said that angels have an angelic party when someone gives their life to Jesus (Luke 15:10). What do you think an angelic party would look like?

Have you ever felt like God doesn't care about you? Do you have doubts and then feel guilty for feeling doubtful?

Do you remember the first time you said yes to Jesus? If you haven't, you can say yes today.

What do you think God is like?

Chapter 7

THE WAITING ROOM

Mom stopped me as I ran toward the door, half a banana crammed into my mouth.

"Momph! Mm gluffah bluh laffah sull!"

"Don't talk with your mouth full, dear."

I swallowed hard. "I'm gonna be late for school!"

I hadn't even heard my alarm go off. Maybe that was because I was so distracted by the same awful dream I'd been having every night. A creepy smile. An outstretched hand. A pulsing seed. Mom grabbed my shoulders and focused me. "Today is Monday. Please remember that you and Grayzon have doctor's appointments today. I need you to walk to the clinic right after school. It's only a few blocks away."

"Aw Mom! Do I have to? We have to sit there waiting forever just so Dr. Hoffman can tell me 'you're as healthy as a mule, Zoe!'... Whatever that means."

Mom crossed her arms, which was a sure sign she was about to win this argument. "Four PM at Dr. Hoffman's. I'll meet you there."

I groaned in defeat. "Fine. Can I go now?"

Mom moved to the side and gestured dramatically toward the front door. "Your chariot awaits, your highness."

I rolled my eyes and ran to the door. I suddenly paused, ran back to Mom, gave her a hug, and then bolted out the door. Sure, she annoyed me sometimes, but that didn't mean I didn't love her. She was my mom, for crying out loud! And family was everything.

I was ready for angels and adventures, but unfortunately the day was uneventful. It was boring, to be honest. I guess after such a crazy weekend, normal life felt so...normal. Teachers helped us learn. Kids joked and played at lunch break. Talia said a couple snotty things to me, but that was it. I kept my eyes open for Joph, but he didn't show himself. At least, I don't think he did. If angels really could be anyone without me knowing, that made me question how I treated those around me. The bell rang, and I wondered about that the whole way to Dr. Hoffman's. Have I ever called an angel a name on the playground? I looked the other way when I passed that guy sitting on the street asking for money—was he an angel?

I got to Dr. Hoffman's office pretty early, and the reception-ist pointed me toward a seat while talking on the phone. She had

perfect blonde hair and plastic-looking skin, which made her look like a real live Barbie doll—except for her goblin-like frown. I sat down as far away from Grumpy Barbie as I could and looked around at the other people: a mother texting on her phone while her daughter played on an iPad beside her, a tall guy in a tie-dye shirt reading a magazine, some old people staring at the wall, a darkly dressed teenager pouting in the corner, and right beside me...a big burly bearded beast of a man, wearing a leather vest with the logo of his biker gang—giant angel wings. He glanced at me out of the corner of his eye, and I chuckled.

"Wow, Joph. Could you be any more obvious?"

The biker raised an eyebrow at me. "Excuse me?"

"Big tough guy, angel wings...you're not fooling anyone, Beardo. Try a little harder with your outfit next time."

The biker frowned. "I like my outfit."

I rolled my eyes. "Alright, alright. Can we just get out of here? We really need to find more of these slimy seeds so we can stuff them up that little demon's nostril. You could just fly us out that window, being an angel and all."

His bushy eyebrows crunched together in confusion. "What the heck are you talking about?"

I looked around, then winked at him. "Oh. Right. Yeah, let's play it cool. You're not an angel." Wink. "You're just a greasy biker dude in desperate need of a bath and haircut." Wink wink.

He growled and got to his feet, towering over me. "Kid, you're crazy. I'm about the furthest thing from an angel." Suddenly his tough demeanor melted, and tears filled his eyes. "But I've still got feelings!" He burst into tears and ran from the room as fast as his burly frame allowed. Everyone in the room watched him go, then looked at me, including Grumpy Barbie behind the reception counter. My face went as red as a tomato and I slid down in my chair, burying my head under my hood. Suddenly my mouth was dry. I took a swig of my water just as the tall man in the tie-dye shirt lowered his magazine and looked at me.

"Wow, that's embarrassing. Talk about a case of mistaken identity."

He winked, and I spewed my water onto my pants, coughing. Again, everyone looked at me, then went back to their own conversations, or devices, or staring at the wall (wow, old people were boring). I mouthed "Joph?" to Tie-Dye Guy, who stifled a laugh and nodded. He casually slid over a few chairs toward me, and I did the same, until we were sitting near each other in the corner of the office. I glared at him. "Why didn't you stop me?!"

"I pick my battles carefully," said Joph. "Don't worry, I just messaged that big guy's angel to come give him some comfort. He's going need it." I groaned and melted even lower in my seat. At least no one else in the room was paying attention to me. Joph snickered and then held up a shining pair of golden shoes.

"Whoa! Are those Yeezys?" I asked.

"Better. They're Jeezys."

I burst out laughing, which earned me another nasty look from Grumpy Barbie. She shushed me and went back to talking on her phone.

"Just kidding," said Joph. "These are a gift to help you walk with confident assurance in who you are and Who you belong to. They're the Shoes of Peace."

"I thought they were called the Sandals of Peace," I said.

"Nobody ever said they were sandals."

I slid the golden shoes on, as they expanded and then collapsed to fit nicely over my sneakers. "A perfect fit."

Joph nodded. "Peace always fits perfectly."

"I could use some peace. I always get anxious at doctors." I thought about the last time I was here. "I've gotten some pretty bad news here."

"I know," Joph responded.

One Year Ago

"So how is he, doctor?" Mom said.

"It's going to be a long recovery," said Dr. Hoffman. "He has three fractures in the left leg and a lot of swelling. You'll have to keep him off his feet for a while."

"Don't worry, I just picked up the new PlayStation for him. He'll forget about his broken leg in minutes," Dad joked.

But I didn't think it was very funny. None of this was funny. I had been sitting in this waiting room for four hours already, with nothing to do but think about what had happened and worrying about whether or not Grayzon was going to be okay. It was my fault he was here. I was the one who dared him to jump from the roof to the trampoline. I was the one who called him a chicken when he wouldn't do it. I was the one who told him nothing could go wrong.

But it did go wrong. Grayzon had landed awkwardly and bounced straight off the trampoline. I could still hear the sickening snap as he landed on the pavement. And I could still hear him screaming as he held his leg and cried.

"Why did you make me do that?!?!"

I was jolted from the memory as someone slumped into the seat beside me. I looked over to see Grayzon flip on his Nintendo Switch.

"Grayzon!" Oh right, he had an appointment too. Mom mentioned that. "Uh...hey."

"Hey," he mumbled. We sat beside each other in silence for what felt like hours. When I looked at the clock, it had only been two minutes. Ugh, waiting was the worst. I was stuck beside my brother who hated me, which only made me more uncomfortable. We used to be best buddies. He was such a fun older brother. And then I went and messed it up. And no matter how many times I said I was sorry, it didn't seem to matter. I was stuck waiting, waiting, waiting for him to forgive me.

Joph, on the other hand, seemed to have no problem waiting. He was slouched in his chair, relaxing with his thumbs in his belt. Hey! I had a belt too! Maybe my Belt of Truth would help me figure out how to get my brother to like me again. Or at least help me understand what his problem was. I concentrated, trying to make it appear. Come on, come on, I need some truth! I thought about Jesus, and how He said in the Bible that He was the Truth. Jesus knew what was going on with Grayzon. Maybe He could help me! And that's when I felt the belt around my waist. Yay! "Jesus," I whispered quietly to myself, "help me to see what's going on with Grayzon." I looked at my brother, but he was so absorbed in his game that he didn't notice. Nothing seemed different. Was I missing something? He leaned over to inspect something on his Switch, and that's when I noticed something peeking out from under his shirt, between his shoulder blades.

It was a fear seed.

I stammered, trying to say something.

"What?" Grayzon hissed, without even looking up.

"I...uh...you've got something on your back."

Grayzon frowned, shook his shirt collar as if to brush off dust, and went back to playing.

"It's, um...there's these things called..." I didn't know how to explain this. "You ever seen a slimy seed before?"

Grayzon double tapped a button and his Switch game made a soft exploding sound. "You're being weird. Stop being weird."

"Are you...feeling okay?"

Grayzon finally paused the game and glared at me, whispering harshly. "I don't want to be here. I especially don't want to be here with you. You may have forgotten, but I haven't."

"I know you're still mad at me. I told you I'm sorry. We could pray for your leg again, if you want..."

Grayzon turned and glared at me. "I tried praying. And I didn't get better." Grayzon rubbed his leg, which had never healed properly. The doctors said he would have a limp the rest of his life. "What's the point in praying anymore? You can't change anything."

"You don't mean that," I said. "You're just scared."

"I'm not scared. Don't be stupid. Look, if you have something to say that actually makes sense, now's your chance." He paused. I glanced at the fear seed peeking out of his shirt collar. I could grab it. Maybe. Was it my fear seed, or was it his? I couldn't decide what to do. Grayzon grunted and went back to his game. "That's what I thought."

I decided to grab it. Joph might be a ninja with feathers, but I had decent ninja skills too. I pretended to stretch, putting my arms above my head, and then began reaching toward his back. I was almost there, when a warty clawed hand grabbed my arm.

Fearmonger stood on the other side of Grayzon, reaching over behind my brother's head. Was it just me, or was he a little bit taller than he was in the Dollar Store? Fearmonger shook his head at me. "Uh uh uh. This boy is mine. I've got my seed buried deep, and you can't have him back."

I was speechless. Was Grayzon being affected by Fearmonger? Was the poison of this demon's words soaking into my brother? I wanted to tackle the little creep, but how would that even work? Was Fearmonger really physically here? What would it look like to everyone else if I jumped at an empty chair, screaming and punching? What would Grayzon think of me? I couldn't do that.

Luckily, I had a guardian angel who was more than happy to punch that ugly little goblin in the face—which is exactly what he did.

"Hands off the both of them!" roared Joph, who tackled Fearmonger to the ground. They began rolling around on the floor, fists and claws flying everywhere. I looked around the room in shock. Was someone about to call the police? A priest? Ghostbusters? But nobody even looked up. Wow. Angels and demons fighting right in front of them, a spiritual battle taking place, and nobody even knew it was happening. And to think—this kind of stuff happened all the time! That's crazy-pants-banana-town.

"Grayzon Narciso?"

Joph and Fearmonger froze, the angel sitting on top of the demon, bending his long nose at a strange angle. My brother and I both looked up to see Dr. Hoffman standing in the doorway. "You're up first." Grayzon got up and shoved his Switch in his backpack. "Your leg looks like it healed well!" Dr. Hoffman said cheerfully. Grayzon had just enough time to glare at me over his shoulder before he walked inside the room. Fearmonger gave Joph the same glare and flew in after my brother as the door shut. Joph was about to take off after him when he saw my sad expression.

"You okay?" Joph said softly, getting up and sitting down beside me.

"I feel like I just got drop-kicked in the heart. I can't believe Grayzon has a seed on him. What's going to happen to him?" I glanced at my new shoes and tapped the heels together. "I sure could use some peace right about now." Tap, tap. "Come on, peace me up!"

Grumpy Barbie gave me another stink-eye from behind her phone. I mouthed "Sorry," which seemed to satisfy her.

"That's not how it works, Zoe," Joph said softly. He leaned his head back and closed his eyes.

"What are you doing?"

"Relaxing. You should try it. Just sit still and listen for a minute."

"I don't have time to listen. Grayzon's got a fear seed on him and these shoes you gave me don't seem to be working. And we've got to hunt down Fearmonger!"

I got a fourth stink-eye from Grumpy Barbie so vicious it could make grass wither and die, but I ignored her. I waited for Joph to respond. Eventually, he opened his mouth to say something, then paused. He closed his mouth. After what felt like forever, he finally spoke, slowly and intentionally. "If you live too fast and too loud, you'll miss what Holy Spirit wants to say to you. Just be patient for a minute. You can't figure everything out in fast forward. Sometimes you have to slow down and let Him guide your thoughts."

I rubbed my temples, annoyed. This was not the advice I was looking for. But I had nothing else to do. Fine. I clenched my eyes closed and sat there, vibrating. My heart beat loudly. My hands fidgeted. I took a deep breath. This was dumb. Another breath. What a waste of time. Five more slow breaths, and I noticed I wasn't vibrating anymore. My hands relaxed. All the thoughts smashing around in my mind slowed down.

"There. Now what?"

"Peace isn't about feeling relaxed," whispered Joph. "It's being totally confident that The Commander's got this. It's pushing everything to the side so that He can speak clearly to you."

I watched in my mind as my thoughts slowed, until they were all floating around like a field full of lazy butterflies. Then the weirdest thing happened. One thought seemed to float past all the rest, right up to the front until it filled my mind.

"What are you thinking about?" Joph asked.

"Nothing really. Just a random picture in my head."

"With The Commander, nothing is random. What do you see?"

"A gate...with a red scarf on it. But I don't think it means anything."

"Maybe. Maybe not. Or maybe it doesn't mean anything yet."

I sat up straight, eyes wide. "Wait, so God can put pictures in my mind all the time? He's always talking to me? I can't believe I don't wait and listen more often!"

Grumpy Barbie got up from her chair and started walking toward me. Uh oh.

Joph continued. "Lots of people forget to wait and listen. But the ones who do it often hear from Him the clearest."

I took a deep breath. "I feel better. Thanks."

"When you wait on the Lord, it's like getting a recharge to your power meter," said Joph. "I carry The Commander's presence with me everywhere I go. I can walk in peace all the time. And you can too, if you want to."

"That sounds awesome," I said.

"You know what else sounds awesome?" said Grumpy Barbie, who was now standing right in front me. I cowered in my seat as she towered over me. "Whispering. Whispering sounds awesome. Please talk quieter." She looked at the seat Joph was in. "Who are you even talking to? You're creeping everybody out, talking to your imaginary friend." She frowned and stomped back to her desk, where her phone was waiting for her. I guess she didn't see an angel or a tall man in a tie-dye shirt, like I did. Huh. I probably looked like a crazy person. Luckily, no one else in the room seemed to be paying attention to me.

Right then, Mom came in and sat down where Grayzon had been sitting. "Hi sweetie. How was your day?" She ruffled my hair playfully, but got her fingers caught and had to tug twice to get free.

"Just another Monday, Mom."

"Where's Grayzon? Is he okay?"

"He's already in with Dr. Hoffman." I paused. "He wasn't very happy to be here with me."

"Oh sweetie." Mom reached to stroke my messy hair, then changed her mind and patted my shoulder instead. "I know he's still upset and says mean things to you." She paused, trying to find the right words. "You know the path from our front yard to the road?"

"Yeah…" I said, not sure what that had to do with anything.

"That path never used to be there. Your father made it when we first bought that house."

"Really?"

Mom nodded. "He wanted to make a way to get to the road quickly, but there was no way. So he got a chainsaw and a shovel and started cutting away at the trees and bushes."

"Whoa, that must have taken forever!" I said.

Mom chuckled. "It sure seemed like it. He got a lot of scrapes and tore a hole in the butt of his pants when it got snagged on a branch. Your father wasn't very good at that kind of stuff, but he refused to give up. He's very stubborn sometimes." She elbowed me. "That's where you get your stubbornness from, by the way."

I elbowed her back. "But Mom, what does Dad's path have to do with me and Grayzon?"

"Sometimes when we have so much hurt and anger in our hearts, it's hard to see any sign of hope that things might get better. But when Grayzon is ready to forgive you, he will start to cut a path through that hurt and anger. That's what happens when we forgive. Does that make sense?"

I tapped my fingers to my mouth as my brain started to slowly put together the pieces, like finishing a puzzle in my mind. "When we forgive…we let go of the hurt and ask God to heal our hearts, to make things new. It might not be easy, and we might get some scrapes and cuts along the way, but with God's help we can cut things off and make a way where there was no way."

Mom grinned. "Exactly!" She ruffled my hair like she always did when she was proud of me, and of course got her hand caught in a big knot of my hair. She quietly worked her hand free, and I tried not to scream out loud in pain. I didn't want to face the wrath of Grumpy Barbie again.

"I'm sorry, honey. For the hair, for how hard it's been with Grayzon, for how tough things have been at school. I know you're trying the best you can. And I know you ask God for help, writing your thoughts in that Beauty Book journal I gave you."

I suddenly felt like guilt had kicked me in the stomach. Mom thought I was writing nice things in that book. But the book didn't say Beauty anymore—it said Bruise. And there weren't very nice things in there at all.

"Hey," she said, grabbing my hand, "when you and Grayzon are done here, why don't we go get ice cream?"

"Really? You're the best!" I exclaimed, hugging her tightly.

"Kid, I said shut it!" hissed Grumpy Barbie, without even looking up from her phone.

"Excuse me?" said Mom, frowning and sitting up straight. "I don't think that's any way to talk to a child." Grumpy Barbie looked up, startled. I guess she didn't know Mom was sitting with me now. I almost felt bad for her—Mom was about to go into Mama Bear mode, and Grumpy Barbie shouldn't have messed with Mama Bear's cub. "We are having a very special mother-daughter moment, which is more important than your silly silence rules, and definitely not deserving of rude comments. Now why don't you stop talking to your boyfriend and actually do some work?"

Everyone else in the room tried not to giggle as Grumpy Barbie's eyes went wide. She looked at the phone in her hand. "How did you know—" she started. She blushed, then whispered quickly into the phone. "I gotta go, Smoochy-Poo." She hung up and began typing, and Mom sat down victoriously. Right then, Dr. Hoffman opened her office door and Grayzon came out.

"So?" said Mom.

"Healthy as a mule!" said Dr. Hoffman. Grayzon and I both rolled our eyes at the same time, then tried not to laugh. It was the first time in a long time that I had seen him smile. That made me happy.

ZOE'S REPORT ON ANGELS

What I learned today (Monday):

· Angels carry God's presence with them everywhere
· Angels are patient
· Angels really don't like demons

DISCUSSION QUESTIONS

Peace is being totally confident that The Commander's got this. Describe a time that you needed shoes of peace to help with your worry.

Think about a time when you asked for someone to forgive you, but they didn't accept your apology. How did that make you feel? Did you know that God forgives you, even though the person didn't?

Chapter 8

GUT FEELINGS

I brushed my teeth while rubbing the sleep out of my eyes and remembered the hand, the seed, the grin. I was getting pretty sick of that dream. I glanced into the mirror and saw my hair, which resulted in me spewing toothpaste all over the mirror. Wow, that's a new trick—scaring myself with my morning hair. I was actually impressed. I cleaned the mirror as I thought how nice it would be to cover up that crazy hair. Oh wait! I had just the thing. The Helmet of Salvation!

I concentrated, willing the helmet to appear. Nothing happened. Huh. I thought it was always with me. I tried again. Nothing. Did I lose it already? I lost a lot of things, but I didn't think I could lose a piece of heavenly armor. Hmm. Maybe the way to make it appear was to remember why I had the helmet. It was a reminder that because Jesus died and came back to life, I have been given new life—salvation. The Helmet of Salvation protects my mind from wrong thoughts, because when I remember what Jesus did for me, that helps me choose good thoughts and say no to the bad thoughts! The memories of my nasty dreams faded away immediately, and I looked back at the mirror. There it was. Sitting on my head, shining from the bathroom lights, covering my hair.

"How do I look, Puddles?" I said, looking back at my frog's tank. She croaked in response. I assumed that meant she liked it. I smiled at myself in the mirror. The armor of God was the best. I wanted more of it! I remembered I also had the Belt of Truth, which I should put on. The best way to do that, I figured, was to get some Truth in me. That meant reading my Bible! I picked up my phone to open my Bible app, and noticed I already had some messages waiting for me. The first was from Aaliyah.

> **FutureMissPresident:**
> Happy Tuesday. Don't forget your science report.

> **BenBen1010:**
> Zoe I saw the funniest squirrel yesterday

Attached to Bennett's message were twelve different videos of the squirrel running around his backyard.

> **Skeeter999:**
> Ugh today is going to suck why bother getting out of bed, amiright?

> **BigGuy:**
> Good morning, Little Warrior.

I frowned and stared at my screen. There was only one person who called me "Little Warrior."

> **WarEagle4Life:**
> JOPH? Are you...messaging me?

> **BigGuy:**
> Trying something new. :)

> **WarEagle4Life:**
> This is weird lol. R we gonna find more seeds today? Cuz I'm fine to skip math class and go hunting.

> **BigGuy:**
> Math first, seeds later.

> **WarEagle4Life:**
> Oh come on...I don't want to listen to Ms. Ratzlaff explain probability today. I don't even know what it is

> **BigGuy:**
> Probability is the chance that something will happen. For example, it is not likely to rain tomorrow, or there is a 70% chance you will forget to eat breakfast.

> **WarEagle4Life:**
> Or a 100% chance that Talia will be mean to me today. See now I know what probability is. I don't need to go to class

> **BigGuy:**
> Nice try LOL. Go learn math. You never know when it might come in handy.

I raised an eyebrow. Angels said LOL? I shrugged.

> WarEagle4Life:
> Fine

> BigGuy:
> See you later. Don't forget to do
> your devotions this morning.

I fed Puddles, read my devotions, put on the Belt of Truth and my Shoes of Peace, and got ready for school. I was so tired that it wasn't until I got to school that I realized my leggings were inside-out today. Hopefully nobody would notice—especially Talia. Luckily, the first half of the school day went by fast with no drama. But all that changed when lunchtime arrived.

Bennett and Aaliyah were waiting for me at our usual eating spot, the little nook near the art room. It was quiet and (most importantly) hidden, so Talia wouldn't find us and cause problems. I was super hungry (because, as Joph predicted, I did indeed forget to eat breakfast). We talked about our weekend and what we picked for our "supernatural creature" assignment. Bennett had picked Pegasus the flying horse from Greek mythology, and Aaliyah had indeed chosen Bigfoot.

"What about you, Zoe?" Bennett asked.

"I picked angels."

"Really? What made you pick that?"

I glanced past them toward the art room, where Joph was leaning against the wall. He waved.

"I guess you could say the inspiration just...appeared out of thin air."

"Well angels should be easy to research," said Aaliyah. "There's lots of cartoons and commercials about those cute little guys, sitting on clouds playing harps."

Out of the corner of my eye, I saw Joph pretending to throw up. I burst out laughing. Aaliyah just looked confused. "What's so funny?"

"Nothing," I said. Joph winked and was gone. "I'm just realizing angels are a lot more...interesting than we assume." As I was chuckling, Karissa walked past us. Our eyes met and my smile faded. Karissa lowered her head and rushed away, accidentally bumping into some other kids.

"What's Crazy Karissa's problem?" said Bennett. "She always acts so weird around you."

I took another bite of my sandwich, ignoring Bennett's question. He immediately moved on and started talking baseball.

After lunch, we went outside to find something to do with the time we had left before next class. A group of kids were playing tag, and since we knew most of them, we joined in. Aaliyah started teasing me when she noticed a short blonde boy kept targeting me. I blushed and told her to stop. Ten minutes later, I leaned up against the fence, puffing as I watched the other kids start another round of tag. The blonde boy jogged up beside me. "You gonna come play again?"

"How do you still have energy? Don't you get tired?"

"Not really. I have the boundless energy of ten thousand puppy dogs!"

I frowned and looked at the kid closer. He had little clouds all over his shirt, and his blonde hair was shining so bright in the sunlight it almost looked like...a halo.

"Wait a minute... Joph?"

The boy laughed. "Took you long enough!" I blinked in the bright sunlight, and when I looked again, he was his usual nine-foot-tall hulking form again.

"So now you're just hanging out with me, playing games at school?" I said. "Or is this part of the mission?"

"Everything I do is part of the mission," said Joph. "Whether I'm fighting for you, comforting you, or bringing you messages to your heart from The Commander Himself, it's all part of the mission."

"And are you going to tell me what your big mission actually is?" I asked.

"What, you haven't figured it out?" Joph smiled. I growled. Angels and their mysteriousness. So annoying. He pointed at me. "Hey, I'm digging your style today."

I rolled my eyes. "Don't make fun of my inside-out pants. I keep forgetting to fix them."

"I wasn't." He tapped me on the stomach with a loud clang. Puzzled, I looked down and saw my chest and stomach were covered with a beautifully decorated golden breastplate.

"Oh snap! The Breastplate of Righteousness! Sweet!" The piece of armor fit perfectly. I took a big breath and was surprised at how safe I felt.

Joph nodded in approval. "This is a visible reminder that you were designed to reflect The Commander, who is completely good, totally perfect, and absolutely right in all He does. That's what righteousness is: 'living right,' choosing to love and obey perfectly."

"Love and obey perfectly? That sounds impossible!"

"Hm, yes," said Joph. "If only there was something that could help us do it...something we could wear to protect our heart...like a piece of armor..."

I shoved Joph playfully. "Okay, okay. I get it. That's what the armor is for, isn't it? To help us, like, tap into God's strength to do things and be something greater than I could on my own strength."

Joph smiled. "Now you're getting it." He tapped the breastplate. "With The Commander's help, you can be a beautiful reflection of Jesus to everyone around you."

My heart felt stronger. As if any bad words spoken against me would just bounce off, like arrows shot at me by an enemy. "Wow. Where has this been all my life?"

"The Armor has always been here, ready for you to put on. You just have to choose to put it on every day."

"Wow, that's pretty awesome of God to protect me like that."

"Yeah," Joph sighed dreamily. "He's the best. Now, we've still got a bit of time before lunch is over. What do you want to do? Math?" He winked at me.

"Ew, no!" I exclaimed. "We could go seed hunting, but I'm not allowed to leave school property. The farthest I could go is that tree." I pointed to a tree across the field. Frankfurter Elementary School and Hamburger Middle School were separated by a big field with a single oak tree right in the middle. It used to be a favorite place of mine, but I hadn't gone near there since I was on the other side of the field, as a grade three kid in Frankfurter Elementary. There were... bad memories over there. "Let's start behind the school," I said.

"What makes you think you'll find anything?" said Joph.

"I just...have a feeling. In my gut."

Joph shrugged and followed me, humming a War Eagles song. We looked for seeds along the front chain-link fence, by the basketball court, behind the school...nothing. I was peeking under some pipes at the back of the school when I groaned in frustration. "Come on! Where is it?"

"You seem pretty sure you're going to find one," said Joph.

"It's school!" I said, banging my head on a pipe. "The scariest place on earth! Of course there's gonna be a seed here." But after five more minutes of looking, I had still found nothing. I grunted and kicked an empty pop can. "I know there's one here somewhere. I can feel it."

"Maybe you just need to take a break," said Joph.

I sighed, and together we found a place on the grass. I looked around. Some kids were playing soccer, some were huddled up watching things on their phones, others were...I froze as I looked toward the big oak tree in the field. Near it sat Karissa, alone as usual. But she wasn't going to be alone for long. Talia and a group of her followers were heading her way.

DISCUSSION QUESTIONS

Zoe tried to "will" the helmet of salvation to magically appear on her head, but soon realized she needed to concentrate on God's Word for it to appear. When you are feeling discouraged, sad, angry, or want to give up, can you replace your bad thoughts with good thoughts from scriptures you memorize? Can you name some scriptures you already know?

Did you know all the pieces of the armor of God before reading this book? Does it help you to better understand the different pieces as Zoe receives each one? Which piece of the armor would you really like to have or know more about, and why?

Zoe hadn't dealt with her bad memories before Joph showed up. Have you ever talked to God about any bad memory you may have? Did you know God cares and can heal your bad memories (1 Peter 5:7)?

Chapter 9

CRAZY KARISSA

I started walking toward the tree. Joph called after me. "Hey, I thought you wanted to go seed hunting!" He was right. I did. But right now, for some reason, I just had to go this way. Talia and her gang had reached Karissa and were talking to her. Their backs were to me, so nobody saw me run up and hide behind the oak tree. I could just hear what they were saying...and it wasn't very nice. I could see Karissa, still sitting on the ground, clutching her backpack.

"She looks terrified," Joph said.

"Yeah."

"Somebody should do something."

"Yeah." I looked up at him. "Maybe you could appear in front of all of them. I bet Talia would pee her pants!"

"Sorry, but this isn't my fight."

"But you're the one dressed for battle!" I said, pointing at his outfit.

"So are you." Joph pointed at me, and I suddenly remembered that I was wearing my armor.

I gulped. "Joph, stopping Talia's bullying would be the right thing to do, but..." I glanced at the tree I was hiding behind, "...the last time I was at this tree with Karissa, I definitely did not do the right thing."

Two Years Ago

I was running as fast as I could. But unfortunately, Talia was faster, and she was gaining on me.

"I'm gonna get you, Zoe!" she yelled. I squeaked in alarm and turned toward the oak tree in the middle of the field, hoping I could get away from her if I could jump into one of the lower branches. As I approached the tree, I held out my hands and prepared to jump. So close, so close...Talia smacked me on the back, making me miss the branch and stumble to the grass. She stood over me, blocking the morning sun. She crouched down, putting her face close to mine...and grinned.

"You're it!" she said playfully and ran back to the tree to stay out of reach.

I got to my feet and brushed at my pants. "Aw, boogers! My mom's gonna be mad about these grass stains. These were my brand-new grade three pants!"

"Well that's what you get for being too slow," Talia teased.

"Time out," I panted, trying to catch my breath. Talia rolled her eyes and climbed into the tree like she did every day. I had met Talia on the first day of grade three. She was new to the school, and since she didn't know anyone, I thought I would be her friend. Lately, Grayzon had been telling me that Talia was a bad influence, but I didn't care. Being her friend was exciting, even if it meant I had to put up with the things I didn't like about her too. Not that I would ever say that to her. Just because we were friends didn't mean she wouldn't knock my teeth out if I told her she was doing something wrong. I liked my teeth and was really hoping to keep every one of them in my mouth where they belonged.

"Are you ready yet?" Talia said, dropping down from the branches. We played near this tree because it was as close as we were allowed to get to all the middle grade kids without leaving school property. Talia was obsessed with older kids and wanted to be just like them. She had even stolen a cigarette from her dad so she could one day smoke it with the older kids who always smoked behind their school. She said I could try it too, but I had smelled cigarette smoke once and there was no way I was going to let my breath smell like burning garbage.

"Can we play something else now?" I asked.

Talia shook her head. "No, I want to keep playing tag. It's my favorite game, and it makes me happy. You want me to be happy, right, Zoe? Isn't that what best friends are for?" she said, holding out her fist. I smiled. We had created our super-secret handshake last week during recess. I fist-bumped her and began the pattern.

Bump, bump, slap, slap, slide, bump, elbows, knees, finger wiggles, bump.

We were giggling so loud that we didn't even notice a girl approach.

"Cool handshake."

We turned to see Karissa, a new girl who had just started at our school this week. Her long blonde hair was half covering the picture on her t-shirt. It was Unicorn Party, one of my favorite TV shows. I was about to say hi, when Talia stepped in front of me and crossed her arms. She wasn't smiling anymore.

"It's secret. Nobody else gets to see it."

"Oh, sorry. I didn't know." Karissa took a breath. "Um, can I play with you guys?"

Uh oh. Clearly Karissa didn't know the rules. You didn't ask to play with Talia. Talia decided every day who got to spend time with her. Luckily, I had been her top pick this whole week. Talia looked at Karissa and snickered. "Why are you wearing a Unicorn Party shirt? Only babies watch that show. Right Zoe?"

My face grew hot. If Talia saw my room, and all the Unicorn Party posters and toys I had, would she make fun of me too? I didn't want her to do that. Sure, Talia was mean sometimes to other kids, but so far, she had been nice to me. I really wanted her to like me, no matter what. Even if that meant not liking Unicorn Party anymore.

"Yeah," I managed to say, "only babies watch that."

Karissa's smile vanished, and she began to scratch nervously at her arm. The peanut butter and jam sandwich I had for lunch suddenly felt like a concrete brick in my stomach.

"See?" said Talia. "Unicorn Party isn't cool. I decide what's cool."

"But..." Karissa was stumbling for what to say. "I have this. It's cool, right?" She held up her wrist, showing us a sparkling pink watch with the "Dream Defenders" logo on it. Talia's eyes went wide. Every nine-year-old loved that book series, even Talia. Her face instantly went from a mean frown to a kind smile.

"Yes, that watch is very cool. But it would look even cooler on me, don't you think, Zoe?" said Talia. Karissa looked at me, confused. Talia crossed her arms and looked at me too. "A real friend would give me nice things. Are we real friends?"

I felt like my heart was playing tug-of-war. I wanted to say no to Talia and let this poor new girl walk away. But another part of me knew that Talia was quickly becoming the most popular girl in school, and if I didn't do what she said I'd get left in the dust, and then nobody would like me. Talia always said being popular was the most important thing in the world. And I couldn't say no to her. I wasn't brave enough to do that.

"You should...give her the watch," I said, although my throat was so dry that it sounded more like a croak. Karissa put her hand behind her back and shook her head. I could feel Talia watching me. If I didn't get that watch from Karissa, Talia might hurt her. I'd seen her hit other kids when they didn't do what she said. Really, making her give the watch was the kind thing to do, because I'd be saving her from a beating. I held out my hand. "If you don't give me the watch, um..." I thought of some way to convince her. "I'll tell everyone that you're crazy. Then no one will play with you, ever. You don't want...um..." I scrambled to come up with a threat that could work. "You don't want to be called Crazy Karissa, do you?"

As Karissa's eyes filled with tears and she slowly took off her watch, I felt like a part of me was dying. She held out the watch to me, but Talia grabbed it from her hand. "Thank you for the watch, Crazy Karissa," said Talia, as she put the watch on her wrist.

"B-but..." Karissa sputtered, "you said you wouldn't call me crazy if I gave it to you."

"No, Zoe said that. I'll call you whatever I want, Crazy Karissa."

Karissa turned and ran. I could hear her crying all the way past the monkey bars. Talia smiled at her new watch and went back to climbing the tree. I told her I needed to go to the bathroom because

I wasn't feeling good, which was true. As soon as I got to the toilet, I barfed twice and then spent the rest of lunchtime sobbing uncontrollably.

I stood there watching Karissa being bullied and remembered how I was once the one doing the bullying. I hurt someone so bad. Could I really fix that? We hadn't talked to each other in two years—her because she was scared of what I might say, and me because I was too ashamed. Every day I pushed down the pain I felt in my heart and ignored her. But I couldn't do that today. I felt different. I felt like I had to do something. Like I was meant to do something.

"Are you okay?" asked Joph.

"I want to help her, but...those kids...and Talia..."

Joph knelt down beside me. "Zoe, I watch everything you do. You turn off your War Eagles music when other kids are around. When people ask what you did over the weekend, you say 'nothing' even though you want to share the cool things that happened at church. You care too much what people think about you. You're trapped."

That got my attention. "Trapped? How am I trapped?"

"The greatest prison people live in is the fear of what other people think. Let me ask you a question—would you rather do the right thing and get made fun of, or do nothing and give up the opportunity to help someone just so you can be like everyone else?"

I didn't know what to say, so I said nothing.

"Zoe, you care too much what people think about you," Joph continued. "The only thing that matters is what The Commander thinks about you. And what He says about you...wow, you have no idea."

"I have a little bit of an idea," I said, thinking back to what I had read in my morning devotions. "In First Peter it says I'm God's chosen treasure. Like, a heavily guarded treasure of heaven."

Joph's eyes lit up. "That's the truest thing you've said all day."

I looked back at Karissa. Talia had just said something that the other kids apparently found funny. This was getting worse. "They're going to say mean things to me, Joph. They already call me weirdo."

"They call you weirdo, because you're not 'normal' like everyone else. But last time I checked, normal isn't working," said Joph. "Maybe being weird is worth it."

"But being weird means people might not like me." I looked at Talia with a deep sadness I had forgotten about. "I don't want to lose more friends. I don't want to be alone."

"Zoe, The Commander isn't going anywhere. And neither am I. I'm going to stay right here, by your side."

"Even when I do stupid stuff?"

"Especially when you do stupid stuff."

I let go of the breath I didn't realize I was holding. My feet were itching to move, and they kicked something. I looked down and saw the fear seed I had been searching for, tangled in the roots of the tree. Of course it would be here, where I had first given in to the fear of being rejected. Duh.

"Hey, you found it!" said Joph.

I was about to grab it when I heard that awful muddy laugh and looked up. Fearmonger. He was darting around the group of kids, poking them with his long pointy nose. Every time he poked a kid, they would say something hurtful. I watched as he grabbed Karissa's shoulders and began whispering in her ear. Nobody else could see him but me. And I knew exactly what he was doing. Sure enough, when he took his hands off her shoulder, there was a small fear seed attached to her. I stared at that group of girls surrounding Karissa, then back at the fear seed, pulsing below me. Before I could talk myself out of it, I started walking toward Talia's gang.

"Zoe, where are you going?" Joph shouted after me. "Your seed isn't over there!"

"No," I said, "but Karissa's is."

"What are you going to do?"

"Stupid stuff, probably." I smirked.

"Well then it's a good thing I'm by your side," said Joph.

I marched straight toward the group of kids, but I wasn't paying attention to any of them. My eyes were fixed on Karissa. I was almost there when Fearmonger appeared directly in front of me, looking at me eye to eye. Yep, he was definitely bigger than before.

"Where do you think you're going? This is none of your business."

I swallowed hard and closed my eyes and whispered a prayer. "God, I know You want me to help Karissa. Help me now."

Fearmonger stepped back as I prayed, as if something was pushing him away. He shook his head and scowled at me. "Listen to me, little girl. What do you think everyone will think about you if you walk over there and—"

"Would you please shut him up?" I said to Joph, who was standing right behind me.

Joph grinned and cracked his knuckles. "I thought you'd never ask." Fearmonger's eyes went wide as Joph pounced on him like a cat on a mouse, and they wrestled across the field. It was about time I let my guardian angel do what he did best—guard me.

I turned my attention back to the group of kids, who still hadn't noticed me. As I approached Talia, I thought of fifteen different insults and nine ways I could hurt her before she could hurt me back. But I wasn't here for Talia. I was here for Karissa. I adjusted my Breastplate of Righteousness and tried to encourage myself. Do the right thing, do the right thing, do the right thing...

"Um, hi Karissa," I said. The entire group turned to stare at me. Hoo boy, here we go. "Do, uh...do you need help?"

Talia glared at me with a look so sour it could make milk go bad in three seconds. "Go away, weirdo." Those words usually hit me right in the heart, but this time it was different. The insult just... bounced off me. The words didn't hurt this time. I didn't even feel like I needed to write about it in the Bruise Book. Huh, how about that? The armor was working. Even though a part of me wanted to yell at Talia to back off, I simply ignored her. I walked past her, and she shoved me. I stumbled but caught myself and kept walking. I knelt down in front of Karissa. I was hoping to see thankfulness on her face, but all I saw was pain.

"Are you here to make fun of me too?" said Karissa. "Or do you just need me to give you another watch?"

Ouch. I deserved that. "No. I just...I know what it's like to get picked on."

"Of course you do," said Talia. "You're a loser. You can't even put on pants properly." All the kids with her laughed. Aw boogers, I knew she'd notice my inside-out leggings. Her words were like arrows, aimed at my heart. But once again, they just bounced off. I could get used to armor like this.

"Karissa..." I paused. This was so awkward with everyone watching, but I knew what I needed to do. "Karissa, I'm really sorry for what I did to you in grade three. That was wrong." I glanced at Talia. "And mean. And I'm also sorry that it took me this long to talk to you again. I guess I've just been so embarrassed. But that doesn't make it okay. Will you..." I sighed, knowing what was about to be chanted at me. "Will you forgive me?"

Karissa stared at me in disbelief, but I saw the corners of her mouth go up in a small smile. It was a beautiful moment until—as I expected—the chanting started.

"Weirdo, weirdo, weirdo!" sang Talia. She was so predictable. Some of the other kids joined in, but I noticed that not all of them did. Some of them had that same stunned look on their faces. Public

acts of forgiveness didn't happen very often at school. I held out my hand to Karissa, and she took it. I pulled her up and we smiled at each other. And then Talia stepped between us.

"Saying sorry is so stupid," declared Talia, puffing out her chest with pride. "I never say sorry for anything, because I don't make mistakes."

I crinkled my nose. "Really? Because I remember you giving one of my dolls a really bad haircut at my house in grade three. You said sorry then."

All the kids turned and stared at Talia. I guess most of them didn't know we used to be friends. Talia's mouth fell open so wide that I could have fit my whole backpack in it. "You can't fix a Barbie with a mohawk, but you can fix a friendship...if you really want to."

As I spoke those words, I wasn't sure if I was talking about me and Karissa or me and Talia. Pfft, yeah right. There was no way Talia and I could ever be friends again.

I prepared for the punch she was about to give me...but it never came. Instead, Talia just turned and stormed off. Not knowing what else to do, the other kids all walked off in different directions, until it was just Karissa and I left. Joph walked up to my side, and I noticed he had scratches all over him. Fearmonger was nowhere in sight. It was hard to tell who had won their wrestling match.

"Thank you," said Karissa. "Why did you help me?"

"Because...it was the right thing to do." I smiled. So did she. "Karissa, I wish I could take back the mean things I said or did to you. But I can't." An idea formed in my mind. I looked at the purple bracelet on my wrist, the one from the Dollar Store that was now a reminder of how wrong choices could be fixed when I owned up to my mistakes. I pulled it off my wrist and held it out to Karissa. "I can't give you back your watch, but here." I put it in her hand. "This bracelet isn't worth a lot of money, but it's really special to me, and I want you to have it."

Karissa admired it quietly, then slid it on her wrist. I was about to say something else, but she wrapped me in a big bear hug so tight I thought I was going to pop. Then she let go, smiled awkwardly, and ran off toward the school. As she did, I noticed something fall off her shoulder into the grass. It was her fear seed, which shriveled away until there was nothing left.

Joph shoved me playfully. "Good job...weirdo."

I shoved him back and smiled. "Her fear seed died! That's awesome."

"So awesome," said Joph. "But what about you? You walked away from your own seed."

"I guess...I guess I wanted to help Karissa more than I wanted to help myself."

"Now that," Joph said proudly, "is a good reflection of Jesus."

I turned and walked back toward the oak tree. But when I got there, I found only a pile of ashes. The seed had crumbled.

"But...how? I didn't do anything to it."

"Yes, you did," said Joph. "You put Karissa first. And when you did that, you were really putting The Commander first."

"Huh. I should do that more often."

Joph smiled at me. And then an acorn bounced off his head. He frowned and looked up in the tree. "Hey! Cloud kisser! You think you've helped your little friend?" yelled Fear-monger, who was crouched on a branch high in the tree. "You've only made it worse."

"What are you talking about?" growled Joph. "Zoe rescued Karissa and repaired their broken relationship. Sounds like a win to me."

"Maybe. But did you see how mad Talia was?" Fearmonger smiled wickedly. "She won't forget what you did, Zoe. She hates you now more than ever. And she's coming for you..."

My knees started to wobble. Oh gosh. It was true. I was in big trouble now. I hadn't even thought about that. "I just wanted to help Karissa..."

"You did the right thing," said Joph. "Don't listen to Fearmonger."

"You didn't help her. Or yourself. Things are about to get so much worse. I own this school!"

Joph started laughing, which shook the fear off of me. Both Fearmonger and I stared at him. "You think you can get in here and hurt these kids? The Commander sends us to every area that is protected through prayer. Zoe's parents pray for her every day, that she would be safe at school and be a light to others. And every time they pray, I'm here to patrol this place and keep things like you out."

"Whoa," I said. "You do that?"

"Yep. I'm your heavenly border patrol agent."

Joph leaned down and whispered in my ear. Fearmonger leaned forward, curious. "What are you saying to her?"

Joph stood up and nodded at me. "Go ahead, Little Warrior. These are words for you to use, directly from The Commander."

"Uh...okay. I have something to say to you, Fearmonger."

Fearmonger chuckled. "Oh, this should be good."

"This school is my school. This school is God's school. I despair—"

"Declare," Joph corrected.

"I declare this is Kingdom territory! Your plans are off-limits! You can't enter here!"

Fearmonger's buggy eyes went even wider. He growled and spit at me. "I can do whatever I want! You think you can beat me? You think this is a battle you can win? I'm going to win this war! Me!"

Fearmonger stomped his feet and said some other terrible words I wasn't allowed to repeat, but I noticed that he didn't come any closer, as if he was stuck in place.

"Well, that was a mistake."

Fearmonger stopped stomping, a confused look on his face. "What was a mistake?"

"Reminding me we're in a war. I'm sick of you hurting people like Karissa and me. I'm a War Eagle, and I'm not gonna bow to you."

The school bell rang, which meant it was time to go back to class. I turned around and walked away from Fearmonger. Joph picked up the acorn that had hit him, aimed carefully, and threw it into the branches above Fearmonger. A pile of acorns bounced down on the demon's head, making him yelp in pain.

"Oops," Joph said innocently. "Did I do that?" He turned and followed me as we headed back inside, laughing all the way.

"Helping Karissa felt good, Joph. I didn't think it would, but it really did." I looked around at all the other kids walking back toward the school entrance. "Maybe...maybe I can help them, too."

"What do you mean?" asked Joph.

"What are the odds that all these kids have fear seeds growing somewhere in their lives? Probably pretty high."

"Interesting. I feel like there's a term for that."

"Of course there is. It's called prob—" I stopped and stared at Joph, who was grinning like a maniac.

"Sorry, what was that?" Joph asked.

I ground my teeth together, forcing the word out. "Probability."

"Huh. Maybe math class isn't useless after all."

I had no witty response to that, so I stuck out my tongue and walked away. Angels could be such show-offs.

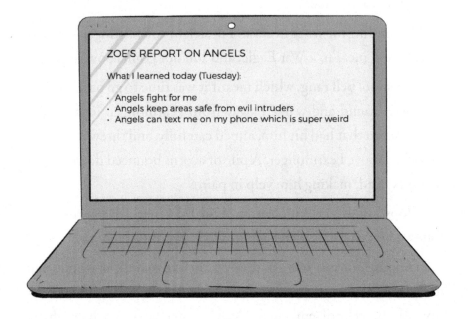

ZOE'S REPORT ON ANGELS

What I learned today (Tuesday):

· Angels fight for me
· Angels keep areas safe from evil intruders
· Angels can text me on my phone which is super weird

DISCUSSION QUESTIONS

Zoe seemed to care too much about what people thought of her. Are you afraid people won't like you if you don't go along with them and do what they want or agree with them? Is this one of your fear seeds?

Several people needed to deal with forgiveness in this story. Do you need to be forgiven for something you've said or done?

Have you ever been mean to someone and then felt sorry (Matthew 7:12)?

Joph helped Zoe "declare" some things straight to Fearmonger's face. Can you think of some things to declare against the enemy you're facing? God's Word works!

Chapter 10

TALIA THE TERRIBLE

I don't know about anyone else, but Wednesdays are the slowest day of the week. Everything moves in slow motion. I dragged myself out of bed and shuffled through my morning routine—brush teeth, shake my head free from stupid Fearmonger dream, get dressed. Today involved trying to find Puddles (who had escaped her cage again). I found her hiding in my left sneaker, as if she wanted to go with me to school. Mom came to give me a goodbye hug and frowned when she saw me.

"Zoe! You've worn that War Eagles hoodie every day for a week. You need to wear other clothes!"

"But Mom, this is my favorite hoodie! I washed it last night. It's clean, I swear!"

Mom frowned but didn't argue back. "Okay, fine. But what about your hair? It's a disaster. Did you even try to brush it?"

"My brush broke last week when I was trying to detach it from my head."

Mom opened the closet and rummaged through a box until she held up a brush exactly like the one I had broken. "Here you go. You know me—I always buy two of everything." I reluctantly accepted the brush and shoved it in my backpack. I grabbed my bike and headed off to school.

The day crawled by slower than a snail in a full body cast. The clock in my class felt like it was frozen in time. I just wanted to see Joph again. I was starting to really like this adventure, as hard as it was. I was ready to crush some seeds and kick some demon butt.

But first, basketball.

The final school bell rang, and the world seemed to return to normal speed. I was the first one into the girls' locker room. I changed into my basketball uniform and was tying my sneakers when Joph sat down beside me. I jumped in surprise.

"I don't think I'll ever get used to having an angel appear before me," I said, trying to calm my racing heart.

"Good," said Joph, "the things of heaven things should never become boring—including angels."

"What are you doing in here?"

"I just wanted to say good luck today. And stay strong."

"Stay strong? It's just a practice."

"That's not what you need to be strong for."

I rolled my eyes. "Everything is mysteries and riddles with you. I'm gonna go. I want to get out of this room before I run into—"

"Hey, weirdo."

Oh no. I looked over my shoulder to see Talia standing in the doorway of the girls' locker room.

"Um, hi." I gulped. I looked back to Joph, but he had vanished.

"Talking to yourself?" said Talia. "Don't think I haven't noticed. You've been acting extra weird this week...weirdo."

"Okay. Thanks," I said and turned toward the door leading to the gym. I ignored her yesterday, I figured I could do it again today.

"Why are you like this?" Talia said, a little louder. Some other girls started shuffling into the locker room and noticing us, including Aaliyah.

I wanted to keep walking, but I was too curious. "Like what?"

"You act like you're better than everyone else," she said, motioning to the other kids. She seemed really mad, for some reason. That did not help to calm all the butterflies in my stomach. A mosquito floated lazily past me as I turned to face her. I was so sick of this, so sick of her bullying, and for some reason I didn't want to put up with it today.

"I don't act like I'm better than anyone!" I said, louder than I meant to.

She waved her hand and motioned toward the gathering crowd of curious kids. "You look at the rest of us like we're not as good as you. You told Brooke you wouldn't listen to her favorite song because it has swear words in it. Prisha over there tried to be nice to you and offered you some of her dad's beer last month. Everyone else tried it. But oh no, not Zoe the Perfect."

My face turned red, and I balled my hands into tight fists. I hated when she called me that. It made me want to punch Talia so hard in her stupid perfect white teeth. I took a slight step forward, but something caught my arm. I turned to see Joph holding my arm. I frowned, holding back tears, but Joph just shook his head and mouthed the words, "Stay strong." How could I stay strong? Her words made me shake like a house of cards, ready to collapse at any second. I thought about how she bullied Karissa yesterday, and so many other kids. She was never going to stop unless someone made her stop!

My brain was buzzing. It was like all the words I had poured onto the pages of the Bruise Book were ready to come out my mouth. Uh oh. This might not be a good thing, but I couldn't stop myself now. "I'd rather be known as Zoe the Perfect..." I took a step forward, ignoring Joph, "...than Talia the Terrible."

All the girls in the room gasped, especially Aaliyah. Everybody called Talia that behind her back, but nobody said it to her face. Talia scowled. "What did you just call me?"

"You heard me." I wanted to shout it with boldness, but it just came out as a whisper. Talia's face went through a series of emotions in a matter of seconds. Surprise, rage, hurt, and eerie calm. I felt a pinch of guilt inside me as I looked at her face. Then, before she could say anything else, I turned and stormed through the door to the gym.

Once practice started, I decided to put all my built-up anger into playing. I ran as fast as I could, shot as far as I could. Three times Aaliyah was open for a pass, but I chose to shoot instead because I was too embarrassed to even look at my friend right now. I ignored Talia, but she was on the other practice team today, so we kept bumping into each other. Halfway through the practice, I got the ball and began dribbling down the court toward the net. Talia stepped out in front of me, and when I tried to run around her, she elbowed me hard in the chest. I flew backward and landed on my back, knocking the wind out of me. I lay there gasping for breath.

Talia leaned over me and whispered, "Get out of my way, or I'll make you move." She flashed me a grin that was almost as nasty as one of Fearmonger's. But I wasn't looking at her face. I was staring at the large, slimy seed poking out from underneath her basketball jersey. It was huge. And pulsing. Talia stood up and trotted away.

How long had that seed been there? She...she had seeds, like me. But her seed was on her heart, and all that fear was eating away at her. I was so deep in thought I didn't notice Aaliyah's poofy cloud of black hair bounce into my view. I could see the disappointment in her eyes as she helped me get up. She didn't mention my outburst at Talia or the selfish way I had acted all practice. She put her arm around me as we walked in silence back to the locker rooms. I guess a good friend knows that sometimes the best thing to say is nothing at all. When I walked out the front door of the school, Joph was standing there waiting for me. I said goodbye to Aaliyah and dragged my feet over to him.

"Hey," he said softly.

"Hey," I replied, not wanting to look him in the eyes. Today had not been my finest moment and being around a warrior of heaven only reminded me how not perfect I was. My phone buzzed, and I glanced at it.

Skeeter999:
Haha great job today! Everyone's talking about how you stood up to Talia the Terrible

I typed a quick reply.

WarEagle4Life:
Well if she didn't hate me before, she definitely does now.

Skeeter999:
She deserved it. Gotta add this 2 the Bruise Book for sure

I paused before responding.

WarEagle4Life:
I don't know

Skeeter999:
Oh come on. Then you can say all the other things you wish you had said to her. Right?

I considered those words, but for some reason the thought of writing in the Bruise Book put a bad taste in my mouth.

WarEagle4Life:
Maybe

Skeeter999:
Hey don't feel bad.

Skeeter999:
We all have different sides of ourselves —nice sides, nasty sides. It's normal...

WarEagle4Life:
gotta go. talk later

I tucked my phone away and hopped on my bike. Joph was already walking away, not even waiting for me. I caught up and pedaled in time with him, not really caring where we were going. As long as it was away from here. "Who was that?" asked Joph, pointing toward my phone.

"Just some kid from my school. Calls herself Skeeter999. Weird name, right?"

"Definitely not as awesome as WarEagle4Life. So, what's this girl like?"

I blushed. "Uh...I don't know. I've...never actually met her."

Joph frowned. "What do you mean you've never met her?"

"She sent me a message on my app last year. Said she knew me from school. We talk all the time. Texts, memes, you know."

Joph raised an eyebrow. "That...sounds suspicious. What do you talk about?"

I shrugged. "Normal stuff. Things that happened in school. How mean Talia is. Stuff like that." I felt weird in my stomach, like I'd just taken a bunch of guilty-pills. "Can we please not talk about this anymore?"

"Sure," said Joph. We turned onto a bike path surrounded by trees. I didn't come this way very often, but I knew it was near the river, which would be relaxing. We moved along for a few minutes until Joph broke the silence. "What happened today?"

Ugh. I knew he was going to make me talk about it.

"I messed up, Joph. I have tried for so long to ignore Talia's mean words, and today I did the exact same thing to her. I thought you're always here to help me. Where were you on that one?"

Joph frowned. "You made it pretty clear you didn't want my help. I won't get involved if you don't want me to."

"I was just so mad, and her words hurt so much."

"Hm. You seemed to do okay yesterday in the field when she tried to make you mad."

"Yeah, but that's because I was wearing—" I paused. "Oh. That's why. I was wearing the Armor of God. But I didn't even think about it today. I'm not wearing my Armor, Joph." I slapped myself on the forehead. "Argh! This was all my stupid fault!"

"Now, now," said Joph. "Don't blame yourself. Putting on the Armor is a habit you have to build, and habits take time."

I was mad at myself. But I was still even more mad at Talia. The mosquitoes were really bad under all these trees. I swatted at one of the little bloodsuckers and huffed. "I'm so sick of Talia. No matter what I do, she keeps saying such mean things about me."

"Like you say about her in your Bruise Book?" said Joph.

I stopped in my tracks and gulped. "You know—wait, of course you do." I shook my head. "It doesn't matter what I write in there."

"Really? You've decided in your heart a lot of things about Talia."

"Well, it's all true!" I blurted. "Everything I say about her is true!"

"Is it?" Joph asked. "True according to who?"

I clenched my jaw. I didn't like this conversation. "You know," I told Joph, "I don't need to say those things about Talia. I don't need my Bruise Book."

"Really? Then why have you been carrying it around with you for the last two days?"

I blushed. He was right. It was in my backpack right now. I had written something about Talia during lunch today because she made me so mad. In fact, my brain had been itching to write about what just happened at basketball practice.

"It's not a big deal. I just write down all the terrible things she's done to me. All her awfulness can literally fill a whole book!"

"You really don't like her, huh?"

"She's a terrible person."

Joph walked back to me and lifted my chin until I was looking him in the eyes. "Zoe, you're no better than Talia."

Those words were like a punch to my gut.

"What? Of course I am!" I shouted. "Talia's terrible! That's why she's called Talia the Terrible!"

I sat down on a log beside the path. Joph sat down beside me. I was so angry. I wanted to keep yelling, but it just came out as a whisper.

"She's terrible."

Joph looked at me with his deep golden eyes. "So are you."

I gasped. I never gasp, but I did then. Joph held up a hand to stop me before I could ask him what the heck he was talking about. "Every person has terrible things inside them. Bad thoughts, selfish desires. No one is truly good on their own."

My face kept scrunching up in anger. "What are you doing? Why are you saying this?"

"Sorry, Little One. But I can only speak truth."

I felt heat rising inside me, from my toes to my messy head of hair. "How is that the truth? I'm not a bad person. I love God."

Joph sighed. "The only thing that can make you a good person is not the fact that you love The Commander—it's the fact that He loves you. But the good news is that He does love you. Which makes you good in His eyes. And if you are good because you are loved, what does that say about Talia?"

"What do you mean?" I asked, not sure I wanted to know the answer.

"Does The Commander love her?" Joph said.

"Yes," I admitted. "God loves everyone."

"And if He loves her, He says she is good in His eyes," Joph said.

I kicked a rock, bouncing it off a tree. My big toe stung from the impact. "No! That doesn't make sense! How can she be good? She couldn't possibly be good unless God took her and, like, rearranged her until she was a completely different person!"

Joph smiled. "Ah, now you're getting it." He patted my knee and stood up. "That's exactly what The Commander does to people who choose to follow Him. He wants to make Talia new, so she can truly be the way He sees her. And you have a part to play in that."

We sat in silence for a couple minutes, listening to the chatter of the birds, until Joph finally spoke again. "Zoe, you are holding on to so much hurt. You need to let it go, because the longer you stay mad at Talia, the longer you'll be trapped."

I thought about that. If I was honest, it felt like there was a hole in my soul from all the pain Talia caused me and the anger I'd been holding on to. Maybe I wasn't any better than Talia. I needed Holy Spirit to heal the hole in my soul so that nothing bad would leak out.

"I'm going to give you a minute," said Joph, who walked down the path until he rounded the corner and was out of sight.

I laid down on the log and looked at the sky peeking through the treetops. I unhooked my silver War Eagles keychain from my

backpack and fidgeted with it as I thought about what Joph had told me. He said God couldn't lie, and angels could only say things that came from God. So, was what Joph said about me true? Was I really as bad as he said? Is that who I was inside? I pulled out my phone and looked at the last thing Skeeter999 had written.

> Skeeter999:
> We all have different sides of
> ourselves —nice sides, nasty sides.
> It's normal...

Nice sides and nasty sides. Was that true? I thought about something we had talked about it in Kids' Church a while back, how we have two parts of us—our spirit and our flesh. Our spirit was our most realest part of us, that connects us to Holy Spirit. Our flesh is all our selfishness and greed and everything bad about us. When I do something kind or generous, that's my spirit! When I lie or cheat or take for myself, that's my stupid awful flesh.

Hm. Maybe there were two parts to me after all. My flesh side, and my spirit side. I felt like my spirit side had been growing bigger over the last few days. My flesh seemed to be getting smaller. But today, I ignored my spirit side and let my flesh side mess things up even more with Talia. I had to trust God to lead me, because I wasn't doing a very good job of leading myself. I couldn't see any way to fix things with Talia and me, but I guess that's what faith was for.

I sighed and sat up. Well, I would have sat up, but some of my hair got caught on the log and it took me two full minutes to get it untangled. I had to use the edge of my War Eagles keychain to saw off a few strands that refused to let go. Finally, I stood to my feet, having only lost a few hairs in my battle with the log.

Joph was right. I wasn't any better than Talia. And I needed to accept that.

DISCUSSION QUESTIONS

Even after Joph warned Zoe to "stay strong," Zoe chose to snap back at Talia. We all have choices every day to do, or say, good or bad things. Can you think of a time when you chose to do or say the right thing? How about when you chose to react the wrong way?

Skeeter999 said it's normal to have different sides of ourselves—nice sides and nasty sides. Do you think it's normal? Can you think of a way to not be nasty, with God's help and your angel's help?

Were you surprised that Zoe didn't actually know Skeeter999? Can you relate to that? How about when you use social media—do you always know who you're "talking" to? You should!

Joph taught Zoe a wonderful lesson in this chapter about truth and how God loves every single one of us, even if we have a nasty side, like Skeeter999 said. How does it make you feel to know that God loves you—all the time—even when you mess up?

Have you ever thought that being a Christian made you a little better than other kids? What did you think when Joph told Zoe she was just as terrible as Talia?

Chapter 11

THE RED SCARF

I walked my bike down the path, searching for Joph. I rounded a corner and saw Joph hovering halfway up a tree. He was talking to a bird. The bird tweeted excitedly and Joph burst out laughing like he'd just heard the funniest thing ever. He saw me, said goodbye to the bird, and floated down to where I was standing.

"Aren't chickadees hilarious?" Joph asked, wiping a tear from his eye. "They always have the best jokes."

I cleared my throat as my shoulders slumped forward. I stared at the War Eagles keychain in my hands so I wouldn't have to look him in the eyes. "I'm sorry for getting mad at you."

Joph grabbed my shoulders and made me stand tall and straight. "I forgive you. But more importantly, so does The Commander."

"Thanks. I feel bad for doubting you."

"Well, it looks like you're choosing faith now, so that's good." Joph extended his hand, revealing a smooth golden shield. "Here, the Shield of Faith will help you with that." The sight of the heavenly object washed away all the worries that had been bouncing around my brain. I grabbed it eagerly and looked it over admiringly.

"Your faith protects you against the attacks of the enemy. Have faith in a loving, perfect God and watch those lies of the enemy bounce off you." Joph smiled approvingly. "Only one more piece to go after this."

As I held it, I felt all the other pieces of armor I'd gathered so far appear on my body. I slid the shield onto my arm and stood proudly, doing my best Captain America pose. "How do I look so far, Joph?"

The gentle giant leaned down and rested his hand on my shoulder. It began to feel warm to the touch, and every piece of armor began to glow brilliantly. Joph stepped back and nodded approvingly. "You were meant to shine, Little Warrior."

I stared into the eyes of this guardian I had come to trust so much in such a short time. We smiled at each other for a really long time. Like, really long. It was starting to get awkward. I was about to say something when Joph spoke.

"Do you really want to know what my mission is?"

My eyes went wide. "Of course I do."

Joph leaned down and booped me on the nose.

My mind went blank. "Me?"

Joph stood up tall and saluted me, standing in soldier-like formation. "Of course. The Commander loves you and will always take care of you and wants the very best for you, as you choose to trust Him. It is my greatest honor to defend you."

"I..." How did I respond to something like that? It was overwhelming. "Thank you." I raised my hand to my head and gave a salute to the hulking orange soldier.

Joph released his salute and turned. "Shall we continue?"

I nodded and took three steps before my breath caught in my throat. The path ahead of us curved around some trees, but a bunch of houses were sprawled out along the path, their backyards ending in fences that ran the length of the path.

The first house on the path had a chain link fence.

The fence had a gate.

On the gate hung a red scarf.

I approached the gate, gently touching the red scarf. Whoa, I couldn't believe it. God put a picture in my head, and now here it was! But what did it mean? Where was I?

"What are you doing?" a voice said in front of me. I jumped, dropping my War Eagles keychain, and looked up to see an older girl standing in the middle of the yard. She was glaring at me as she held her phone up to her ear. Uh oh. Perfect blonde hair, plastic-looking skin, and a goblin frown. Not her. This was bad news.

"I'll call you back, Smoochy-Poo," said Grumpy Barbie, ending her call and crossing her arms. I gulped and wondered if she remembered me. "I remember you," she said, frowning and taking a step toward me.

Aw, boogers.

"Um, I'm sorry," I stammered. "For being loud in the doctor's office and for my mom embarrassing you and for being at your house. I didn't mean to, I was just...looking." I pointed at the scarf.

"Well, go look somewhere else. This is my house, not a museum."

She didn't have to tell me twice. I hopped on my bike and pedaled as fast as I could around the corner of the path. Young adults were intimidating no matter what, but a young adult yelling at you was just terrifying. I had just gotten behind a cluster of trees when I heard Grumpy Barbie yell again.

"What do you think you're doing?"

I glanced over my shoulder to see if she was talking to me, but all I saw were trees. She couldn't see me. Who was she talking to then? I creeped back to the edge of the trees and peeked back down the path. Grumpy Barbie was standing at the gate, arms crossed in frustration. Whoever she was yelling at was still around the corner.

"You were supposed to be home twenty minutes ago. You think you can show up whenever you want?" said Grumpy Barbie.

I heard a quiet voice respond, "Sorry."

"Sorry," Grumpy Barbie repeated, mocking the other person. "Saying sorry makes you sound weak. But I guess that's what you are, little sister. Weak." Grumpy Barbie pointed at the red scarf. "Get rid of this thing. It's starting to attract neighborhood kids."

"But, I just—"

"I know what you're doing. Quit putting Dad's stuff out here. What, you think you can signal him to come home?" She pulled the scarf off the gate and threw it on the ground. "It's not a bat-signal, dummy. He's not Batman. He doesn't care about you. Nobody cares about you."

My face was getting hot. How could Grumpy Barbie talk that way to her own sister? Grayzon and I fought too, but brothers and sisters should never say terrible things like this. It was like pouring poison right into someone's heart. I wanted to scream at her and protect the poor girl she was yelling at. Grumpy Barbie huffed in frustration. "I'm going to work. Make sure the house is spotless before Mom gets home." She stomped away from the gate onto the path toward the girl. "Get out of my way, or I'll make you move," she ordered.

Where had I heard that phrase before?

Grumpy Barbie walked out of my line of sight. Everything was quiet until the other girl shuffled into my view and grabbed the scarf from the grass. When she stood up again, I could see her face.

It was Talia.

And she was crying.

Oh snap. Grumpy Barbie was Talia's older sister? I remember Talia telling me how mean her older sister could be; I just didn't realize it was this bad. How had she put up with her for so long? I wiped a tear from my eye and looked at Joph. The angel had tears in his eyes too, which somehow made him look even stronger.

"She...she looks so sad," I said to Joph. "I didn't know her dad wasn't living with her anymore. That would be awful."

"Zoe," Joph whispered gently, "did you think you were the only one hurting?"

My heart felt like someone was squeezing it really hard. My emotions usually wanted me to do a lot of things to Talia—punch her, yell at her, light her shoes on fire when she wasn't looking...but right now all I wanted to do was hug her. Looking at her as she clutched her dad's scarf, I didn't see Talia the Terrible. I saw Talia, who used to be my friend. And I realized that the feeling I had when Karissa was hurting was the same feeling I was having now. I wanted to help Talia, but...

"I can't help her, Joph. I've tried. She doesn't listen to me. She hates me."

"But once upon a time, she didn't," replied Joph. "Fear seeds aren't the only things that grow in people, you know. The Commander plants seeds as well—life seeds."

"Really?" I said, surprised.

Joph nodded. "All the times you've tried to be kind to her, all the times you tried to show her a good example...you weren't wasting time. You were helping The Commander plant life seeds in her heart. Zoe, you might be the only one who can help Talia. She needs you to get in her mess."

"She's not going to like that."

"I know. But that doesn't mean she doesn't need you."

I grabbed my head. "Ugh, there's like a million thoughts smashing around right now."

Joph tapped me on the shoulder, and then pointed up. Oh, right. I closed my eyes and took some slow, deep breaths. "Holy Spirit, I need Your help." As I waited in silence, I opened my eyes and watched Talia walk toward her house. A little ball of fur came bounding out the back door and jumped at her. She grabbed her dog and went inside, petting its head gently. Huh. I didn't know Talia could be gentle.

"So?" Joph asked. "What did He say?"

"Nothing," I said, disappointed. "I can't hear anything. I've just got a War Eagles song stuck in my head."

Joph raised an eyebrow. "Which song?"

"The same one you've been humming all week. 'Wrap Myself in God and Fly.'"

"Ah yes," said Joph, "that one's a classic." He pulled out his sword, held it like a guitar, and began to sing excitedly.

> I'll bring deliverance to tortured captives
> I won't surrender to the fear around me
> The odds aren't good, but I won't be rattled

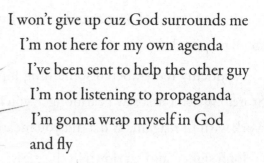

I won't give up cuz God surrounds me
I'm not here for my own agenda
I've been sent to help the other guy
I'm not listening to propaganda
I'm gonna wrap myself in God
and fly

I laughed as Joph pretended to play guitar on his sword and danced across the grass. But as I watched him, I thought about those words. I knew that God wants everyone who loves Him to help bring freedom to others. Talia needed freedom right now. She was hurting, and that's probably why she was such a bully. My kids' pastor once told us, "Hurting people hurt people."

"I want to wrap myself in God and fly," I said, causing Joph to stop dancing. "I want to obey God when He tells me things in my heart, like finding that red scarf. I don't want to give up or listen to plop and grammar."

"Plop and grammar?" asked Joph. "Do you mean propaganda?"

"Yeah, that's what I said. Pop and grandma."

Joph chuckled. "Close. It's propaganda. Propaganda is a weapon that Fearmonger uses to trick people. He spreads lies through other people, and the TV, and your phones." I instinctively touched my pocket where my phone was as Joph pounded his fist into his hand. "I really want to squash that little demon. He's been using fear seeds and propaganda for so long. He's tricked and hurt so many people."

I suddenly remembered something Joph had said in the Dollar Store. "When I first saw Fearmonger, you told him you would never work with him again. What did you mean?"

Joph sighed and sat down in the grass. "There are different kinds of angels, Zoe. Some of them are fallen angels."

"What does that mean?" I said, sitting down beside him.

"Who is our enemy?" asked Joph, plucking a fluffy dandelion and admiring it.

"The devil. Lucifer," I said, although I didn't like talking about him.

"Yes. Lucifer tried to become greater than The Commander and gathered some other angels for battle."

"Whoa! God and the devil fought?"

Joph laughed. "I wouldn't call it a fight. Nobody can match the power of The Commander. Lucifer immediately got kicked out of Heaven, and all his fallen angels went with him. Now you call them demons. They have no love in them. All they have is hate, and they want to hurt The Commander. They know the only way to do that is to hurt His kids. So, they try to trick you and lie to you and keep you away from your Heavenly Father." Joph blew on the dandelion and hundreds of white floaties blew off across the field, leaving it bald and lifeless.

I gasped. "Fearmonger was one of those fallen angels, wasn't he? You guys used to be in God's army together!"

Joph nodded. "I'm very sad he made that choice. How could anyone turn against The Commander?" Joph sighed dreamily. "He's the best."

"Whoa. I can't believe Fearmonger did that. I always thought angels had to do the right thing, no matter what."

"Whoa whoa whoa. You think I'm some kind of heavenly zombie? No way. The Commander gave everyone the ability to make their own choices, including angels. I could walk away from all this too. But why would I ever want to? And why would you? Think of all that The Commander has been doing in your life this week. Freeing you from fear and pain, giving you strength and peace."

It was true. God had been doing a lot of things in my heart and helping me understand. I sighed. "I wish everyone could have an angel like you, Joph."

"Oh, Little Warrior...they do."

My eyes went wide. "You mean, there's like a lot of you?"

Joph smirked and pointed behind me. "You could say that."

I turned around... and gasped. There in the sky was an army of angels as far as I could see, standing at attention, ready to fight. Heavenly beings of every shape and size, with a rainbow of colored skin and glistening armor. It was the most beautiful and terrifying thing I had ever seen.

Joph put his arm around me and waved at the enormous army. "Thanks, guys!" The angel army disappeared, but I could still feel the power that had been radiating from them. After all, they carried the presence of God with them.

"Wow," I whispered, thinking about the amazing image I had just seen. "God has a whole army protecting His kids..."

"Yeah," Joph sighed dreamily. "He's the best." He put his arm around me and pulled me back onto the path. "Come on, Little Warrior. Let's go home. Tomorrow is another chance to change the world."

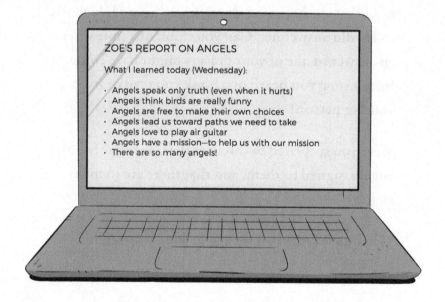

ZOE'S REPORT ON ANGELS

What I learned today (Wednesday):

· Angels speak only truth (even when it hurts)
· Angels think birds are really funny
· Angels are free to make their own choices
· Angels lead us toward paths we need to take
· Angels love to play air guitar
· Angels have a mission—to help us with our mission
· There are so many angels!

DISCUSSION QUESTIONS

Do you ever feel like you're the only one with problems or the only one hurting inside? Is there someone you know who has problems that you can help plant a "life seed" into?

Zoe asked for Holy Spirit's help, but felt like He didn't answer back. But the song she heard in her head that she hummed all week was from Holy Spirit, so He did answer her. Can you think of a time when an answer to one of your prayers might have come from a song you heard or a book you read or from another person?

Were you surprised to discover that everyone has an angel assigned to them, and that there are so many angels?

What do you think it means to wrap yourself in God and fly?

Chapter 12

REVELATIONS

It was now tomorrow. And I didn't feel ready to change the world.

Thursday mornings meant Dad made waffles for breakfast, which normally made my morning awesome. But I didn't feel awesome. All I could think about was the dream I had been having every night—Fearmonger holding the seed. But last night had been different. This time Talia had been in the dream too. And I had realized, with a chill, that in the dream Fearmonger wasn't holding out a seed to me. He was holding it out to scared, lonely Talia. I finished my waffles, but I couldn't even taste their awesomeness.

Once I got to school, I avoided Talia all day because I honestly had no idea what to say to her. She still acted like her usual mean self, but I couldn't look at her the same way I used to. I kept seeing her crying and holding her dad's scarf. The whole day passed by with me in a haze, distracted and uncertain. The only highlight of the day was the fact that I asked Karissa to join me, Bennett, and Aaliyah for lunch, and she did! Bennett and Aaliyah teased each other like they always did, and I laughed at their silliness. Karissa smiled a couple of times but didn't say much. Still, it felt really nice to have her with me.

When the final bell rang, I walked out the front doors with only one goal in mind—a big bowl of Fruitee-Os and an episode of Unicorn Party. (Yes, I still liked that show.) Who was I kidding? I couldn't change the world. And I certainly couldn't help Talia. I joined the crowd of other kids and walked away from the school staring at the ground, hunched over to hold up my insanely heavy backpack. I was deep in thought trying to understand why on earth we needed so many textbooks when I ran straight into someone. I fell backward and landed on my butt with a grunt. A shadow loomed over me, and I flinched when I saw who it was. Aw, boogers. Of all the people to collide with, why did it have to be her?

"Get out of my way, or I'll make you move," said Talia, quoting her sister's awful words. She looked like she had been waiting for me. Uh oh. This wasn't good. I stood up slowly and looked her in the eyes. I realized I didn't feel mad at her...I felt sad for her. I guess Talia could see the sadness in my eyes. "Aw, is Zoe the Perfect going to say sorry again? Sorry, sorry, sorry." Talia smiled, and a few kids laughed as they stopped to watch. Crowds always seemed to gather when it looked like a fight was going to happen. "You're so weird. You've always been so weird." Talia began circling me, taunting me. I had nothing to say, so I just stood there and let her talk. "You never do what everyone else does. You stay quiet when others complain. You stay in the corner when everyone else is having fun." She leaned close. "I hate your perfect attitude, your perfect grades, and your perfect family."

Oh my gosh. That was it. That was why she hated me. That's why she called me Zoe the Perfect.

Two Years Ago

It had been a couple of weeks since I accidentally created Crazy Karissa's nickname and ruined her life, and things seemed to be fine again with Talia. In fact, things were so good she decided she wanted to sleep over at my house! My parents were excited for me to bring a friend from school over, but Grayzon wasn't so sure.

"Talia? Isn't that the mean little girl you always run around with at recess? I know her older sister, and she's really mean, too. I've heard their whole family is mean."

"Grayzon," said Dad. One word was enough to make my brother stop talking.

"Talia's not mean!" I said defensively. Grayzon just raised an eyebrow. I sighed. "Well, sometimes she can be really nice...when she wants to be."

"You know what?" said Mom. "We would love to have her. Maybe she just needs to see some love in action. We've got lots of that around here to give away."

I rolled my eyes. My mom could be so lame. But she said yes!

When Saturday afternoon rolled around, I was so excited. Talia had never been at my house before, and Dad said we could sleep in my playhouse in the trees. I was so excited! I carried out sleeping bags and pillows to the cute little shack and began laying out my favorite toys. As I pulled my "Dream Defenders" dolls out of the toy box, a Unicorn Party sticker fluttered to the floor. I yelped and scooped it up into the garbage. I thought I had gotten rid of all my Unicorn Party stuff! I couldn't let Talia see that.

Talia arrived and was very polite to my mom and dad, which kind of surprised me. Grayzon frowned at her from the couch, and she frowned right back. We played in the playhouse until supper; giving bad haircuts to Barbies (which Talia apologized for) and watching weird videos on Talia's iPad, which had been a gift from her dad. She told me that her dad used to always give her gifts, but he hadn't done it in a long time. Her eyes got glassy until she noticed me looking at her. She sat up straight and told me to stop looking at her weird. We played quietly until supper was ready. As we sat down to eat, Talia looked at her plate and scrunched her nose.

"What's this?" she whispered to me.

"It's adobo. It's a Filipino meal."

"It smells weird."

"No way, it's awesome. Just try it. You'll like it."

Talia picked some up and was about to taste it when Dad held out his hands. "Let's pray."

"I want to pray!" said Grayzon excitedly. He always wanted to pray.

My family joined hands like we always did, and Talia looked around in confusion before she finally grabbed the hands reaching out to her. As Grayzon prayed, Talia looked like she was trying not to laugh. I guess her family didn't pray at their house. We ate our meal and talked about our day. Mom and Dad included Talia in the conversation and asked her so many questions it was embarrassing. I could tell from Talia's face that she wasn't used to getting this kind of attention from adults. Dad said something about how much he loved Mom, and Mom kissed him. Grayzon and I both yelled at them to stop because kissing was super gross, but we both secretly liked it when they loved each other.

Once supper was done, we journeyed through the path to the playhouse. Talia was unusually quiet. I grabbed a Dream Defenders doll and held it up to Talia, hoping it would cheer her up, but she didn't take it. She was looking at a brown journal on my sleeping bag with the words Beauty Book written on the cover.

"Oh, do you like it?" I asked, handing it to her. "My mom just gave it to me as a gift. She said I can write all the nice things I notice every day, because there's so much beauty in the world."

"Why do you guys pray?" Talia said sharply, tossing the journal onto the old wooden floor.

"Uh...I don't know. It's suppertime. We pray at supper."

"It was weird. Your dad kept thanking 'God' for all these things and for blessing you guys. Don't you think that sounds like bragging?"

I put down the doll and sat on my sleeping bag. "Not really. We're just thankful."

"Thankful," said Talia. She seemed really mad all of a sudden. Like, way more than she normally was at school. "Of course you're thankful. For your perfect parents who love each other. For your perfect room and your perfect toys. For your perfect weird food and your perfect invisible God. Everything is just perfect for you."

What was happening? I slowly reached for my favorite stuffie, a cute little angel with a harp and diaper. I put it on my lap and hugged it. "Are you okay, Talia?"

"My family never..." Talia caught herself and turned away from me. I realized that Talia had never really told me about her family. I was surprised when tears formed in Talia's eyes. I had never seen her cry. "I don't like you anymore," she said, snatching her backpack.

"W-what do you mean?" I stammered. "I'm your friend."

"No you're not. You're just...Zoe the Perfect."

The words felt like a punch to my heart. "Why are you acting so terrible?" I asked.

"Maybe that's just who I am," she whispered.

Dad suddenly swung open the playhouse door, phone in hand. "Hey, do you girls want to see a video of a sweet trick shot I just did?"

Talia made up a lie about not feeling well and needing to go home, then stomped angrily out the door and down the path, twigs breaking loudly under her feet. Every snap of a branch felt like a piece of our friendship breaking apart.

"Zoe, is everything okay?" asked Dad.

No, I thought. "Yes," I said.

He gave me a hug, said something I didn't hear, and went back to the house. I stared down the path, more confused than I had ever felt in my whole life. Something hopped up onto my shoulder and I looked over at Puddles, staring at me with her big, cute eyes. I wanted to ask her how she got all the way out here, but I couldn't say anything.

A mosquito buzzed in from the open window, and Puddles tried repeatedly to catch it. I grabbed the journal off the floor, staring at the words Beauty Book written on the front. A sadness grew inside of me where Talia's words had hit me so hard. It was like a bruise was growing on my heart. Talia really was terrible. I grabbed a marker, scribbled out the word "Beauty," and wrote "Bruise" above it. I opened my new Bruise Book to the first page and started to write.

Talia stepped toward me and pointed. "I don't like your super-holy attitude. None of us do. And I'm going to stop you from wrecking our fun with your Jesus-talk. It's like, my mission."

Mission.

Joph talked about mission. His assignment, his purpose. What was my mission?

Then I realized...my mission was standing right in front of me, tearing me apart with her words. I slapped at a mosquito near my neck as a million ideas ran through my mind. I saw myself give her an epic roundhouse kick to the face as the crowd cheered. I saw myself snap back at her with the best comebacks ever as she crumpled to the ground crying in defeat. I saw a thousand ways to get revenge. But all of them felt like poison in my gut. Only one thought didn't make me feel sick, even though I knew it would be hard. The best choices were usually the hardest, I realized. So, I forced myself to do it. I took a deep breath, and spoke not just to Talia, but to all my classmates. "I know you think I'm weird, and different. And to be honest, I am different. I make different choices; I believe different things. But I don't think I'm better. I realize now that I'm no better than anyone else. What makes me different is that I believe there's Someone who is better, and He loves me enough to help me be different and make wise choices." I looked at the sea of faces surrounding me. I saw shock, confusion, or doubt on many of them. But a few faces had small smiles of understanding. That would have to be enough. "I can't change you, Talia. I can only change myself."

Talia stared in shock for a few long seconds. Then she seemed to remember she was surrounded by kids who were all watching her. She laughed and pulled out her phone. "Whatever, Zoe the Perfect. Maybe I should flatten you right here and take another picture for everybody to laugh at."

"You want me to pose for a picture?" I said, feeling done with this conversation. "Here's one of me walking away." I adjusted my heavy backpack, turned on my feet, and took off before she could say another word. I tried to walk as calm as possible, even though I expected her to blast me with a bazooka or throw man-eating tigers at me or whatever super-villains like her do. But nothing happened, so I just kept walking. One foot in front of the other. And with each step, I felt a little lighter and breathed a little easier. Those Shoes of Peace were really living up to their name right now.

"See?" Joph said, appearing beside me. "That armor sure comes in handy."

"That was terrifying," I said, once we were out of sight of Talia and the crowd.

"You did great! I was right there, cheering you on." Joph shot out his arms, his hands now somehow holding pom-poms. He danced and shouted, "Zoe, Zoe, she's our girl! If she can't do it, I guess I'll hurl!"

I groaned. "Keep working on your cheers, Big Guy."

I sat at the table, looking at my family. Dad kept teasing us, never knowing when to stop. Mom talked too much and didn't let us answer questions she asked us. Grayzon mumbled responses and wouldn't look anyone in the eye. I don't know what Talia was talking about—my family wasn't perfect. No family was perfect. But family was still everything.

"Earth to Zoe!" said Dad, startling me and making me drop my fork. Grayzon laughed. Normally I would shoot him a mean look, but I remembered I was wearing the Breastplate of Righteousness and decided to laugh with him instead.

"Huh? What? Sorry, I wasn't listening."

"I was asking you how your day was."

Crazy, I thought. "Normal," I said.

"That's not what I heard," said Grayzon. "I heard you and Talia got in a fight today."

Now it was Mom's turn to drop her fork. "What?"

"We didn't get in a fight!" I said quickly. "She was just..."

"Being Talia the Terrible, like always?" said Grayzon.

"She was just having a bad day. That's all," I said, immediately wondering why on earth I just defended Talia.

"Every day is a bad day for her."

"Well, maybe it's because she doesn't have an awesome family like I do. My awesome parents," I dared to look Grayzon in his eyes, "and my awesome brother."

Grayzon made the same face someone makes when they smell really stinky socks.

"Who knows?" I said. "Maybe even Talia can make a new path. With God's help, anyone can make a way where there was no way." I glanced over at Mom, who winked at me.

Grayzon just shook his head. "You're crazy. Sometimes people are just awful people, like Talia. Nothing can change that."

"Grayzon, that is some stinking thinking you've got going on," said Dad. "Sounds like you need to capture that thought and make it obey Christ."

I chuckled. "Dad, we know! You tell us all the time. We get it."

Dad looked at me. "Do you, though?"

"Sure," I said, stuffing some adobo in my mouth. "When bad thoughts come in my head, recognize them, grab them, and tell them they have to listen to Jesus now. And if they aren't good thoughts, they need to go away."

"Huh. Okay, maybe you do get it. Also, don't talk with food in your mouth."

"Yes sir," I said with a mouth full of food. That earned me a frown from Dad and a laugh from Grayzon. The rest of supper was relatively quiet, except for when Puddles (who had somehow escaped her cage again) jumped up on the kitchen table and made Mom scream. The rest of us laughed so hard we started to cry. I plopped Puddles into the hood of my War Eagles hoodie and finished eating. After supper was done and we had helped clear the table, I poked my head into the living room where Mom and Dad were relaxing.

"Mom, is it okay if I go for a bike ride before homework?"

"Be back in an hour. And don't forget your helmet. You don't need any more scars," she said, without looking up from the book she was reading.

"Mom! My head will be fine. I always wear my helmet..." I winked at Joph and whispered, "...of Salvation." We both giggled for a moment, then Joph quickly stopped.

"But seriously," he said, "obey your mother. Wear your bike helmet."

My smile vanished. "Ugh, fine." I put on my shoes and grabbed my bike helmet from the coat closet. Grayzon stopped me by the front door.

"What are you doing?" he said.

"I'm going to go for a bike ride. I've got a lot of thoughts bouncing around in my brain, and I think I'm gonna go pray for a bit."

"Why did you defend Talia earlier?" Grayzon said. "And why did you say that nice thing about me? And why are you going to pray when nobody's even making you? Something's different about you lately. You're being—"

"Weird?" I said, walking out the door. "I know. Get used to it."

DISCUSSION QUESTIONS

Zoe realized in this chapter that her mission involved Talia. Does this help you to understand that we all have our own individual missions, or destinies, in life? What do you think your mission or purpose might be?

Zoe spoke to her classmates about the Lord. Do you think you could do that someday? Have you already done that?

Zoe's brother, Grayzon, noticed a difference in Zoe. If you changed your ways to more reflect God, who do you think would notice the big change in how you act? Why?

Have hurtful things ever been said to you? What can you do about it?

Chapter 13

THE FOREST OF FEAR

The sun was setting behind the trees as I walked my bike into the entrance of the path. I hadn't even made it ten feet before I smacked my head on a branch. "Ow!" I said, plopping my bike helmet on my head.

"I told you listening to your mom was a good idea."

I stuck out my tongue at the angel as we walked and immediately ran into another branch. Luckily, this one didn't hurt because of my helmet.

"So, what are we doing?" asked Joph as he walked along behind me.

"I don't know. I have so much in my head and my heart. And I don't know what to do with it all." We entered the clearing and I looked over at my playhouse, covered in cobwebs and leaves and vines, unused and forgotten. I had never wanted to play in that little shack again after that awful day with Talia. I squinted my eyes and looked closer at the vines. Those weren't vines. They looked like roots. I followed the roots back to their source and saw a seed, nestled in the grass near the front corner of the playhouse. Of course there would be a fear seed here. This is where things started to go wrong with Talia. I stood over the seed for a long while, wondering what I should do.

Pray about it.

The thought bumped to the front of my mind, just like it did the night I wrote in my Bruise Book asking for help. It had felt like someone had whispered the thought into existence. I realized now that's exactly what was happening. God was speaking to me, and I was getting better at recognizing His voice.

"I think I'm going to pray now," I said.

"I think that's a great idea," said Joph.

Hmmm, where to start...Did I focus on my problem? The seed, Talia, Fearmonger? I looked at Joph and realized how to start. I bowed my head and closed my eyes. "God, thank You for sending me help. I want to trust and obey You, even when it's hard. I know I'm not perfect, but You are. Keep doing good things in my heart." I clasped my hands together a little tighter as I considered what to say next. "And also, please do good things in Talia's heart. It must be so hard for her to not feel safe with her family. I believe You love her so much. Help her get to know You. Um...amen."

"Wow. That was powerful."

I frowned. "Really? I didn't even know what to say."

"Every prayer is powerful, Zoe."

I glanced at the fear seed at the base of the treehouse, expecting it to crumble to dust. But it was still there. Nothing had happened.

"Huh. I did what God wanted. I prayed for Talia. I obeyed. I thought that would destroy the seed. I thought it would be easy."

Joph's smile faded. "Oh, Little Warrior. Obeying The Commander is good, but no one ever said it was easy. Prayer is only one part of getting into the mess of people's lives."

"Oh," I said, feeling the weight of that truth. "Well...I still want to obey anyway. No matter how messy I have to get. No matter how many seeds I have to smash. You're guarding me. God's guiding me. And I'm going to follow."

A slow clap broke the silence.

"Beautiful. Really moving. Touching, even," said the muddy voice I'd come to know and hate. Ahead of us on the path, Fearmonger clapped his warty claws together. "But I'm afraid this is as far as you go, Little Failure."

I stared at him in shock. He was huge—almost as big as Joph! "How are you so—"

Joph interrupted me. "Don't focus on him, Tiny Champion." He jumped up to face the demon. "Walk away, Fearmonger. I shut the mouths of lions a long time ago; I can shut your mouth too."

"Try it, Cupid!" bellowed Fearmonger, flexing his huge arm muscles. "I grow stronger every second! Nothing can stop me now!"

I stood and hid behind Joph, poking my head out to stare at the huge ugly monster. "He's so big..."

"Don't believe the things he says, Zoe. Or the things he shows you." Joph looked at Fearmonger again. "We will not tolerate your lies any longer. Zoe belongs to The Commander, He is happy with her, and He loves her!"

"Why should He love her?" Fearmonger screamed, slobber flinging from his pointy teeth. "It's not fair! I was better than her! I was beautiful and powerful! Look at me! Look what He did to me!"

"You did it to yourself, demon. You spit in the face of The Commander and chose your own fate. You have no one to blame but yourself. I wish it had been different. I wish you would have loved Him as I love Him. But you made your choice, and it's time you accept that."

"I will never accept that!" Fearmonger sneered, pointing at Zoe. "You say she makes Him happy? I don't want that Guy in the sky to be happy! And I'll do everything I can to ruin His fun." I noticed then that he was holding something behind his back. "You think one nice prayer can help Talia? What about all the other awful things you've said about her?"

"That was before," I said. "Things will be different now."

"Oh yeah?" Fearmonger sneered. "What happens if I show her this?" The demon held up a brown leather object with a gold strap around it. I didn't recognize it at first, because the cover had a slimy misshapen seed on it, with roots reaching out across the cover. I could barely read the words underneath the seed. Bruise Book.

I gasped. That monster had been in my house? "How...why do you have my journal?"

Fearmonger ignored me and opened the book. He cleared his throat and read.

"May 28. Talia embarrassed me in front of the whole class during gym. She nailed me in the head with a dodgeball and made me cry. She got all her friends to chant 'crybaby' until I ran out of the room."

Fearmonger looked up at me. I was trembling. He continued.

"I wish I had a thousand dodgeballs so I could smash each one of them in her stupid face. I hate her so much. I wish she were never born."

Fearmonger shut the book and stared at me. "I wonder what our friend Talia would say if she read that? What would she think of you?" He gasped dramatically and pointed to the sky. "Or even worse—what would she think of You-Know-Who? You are a terrible reflection of Him, don't you think?"

He wasn't wrong. Those words were weapons, and if Talia read them, she would never forgive me. Her anger would blow up, I'd be caught in the explosion.

Joph took a step forward and cracked his knuckles. "Don't talk to her like that."

"Yeah," I said, gathering courage as I remembered the heavenly guardian standing beside me. "I'm not going to listen to you."

Fearmonger cackled. "Of course you are! You've been listening to my voice for years."

"What? No I haven't, I just met you."

"Oh really?" Fearmonger leaned forward and whispered. "Because I'm pretty sure I've been constantly buzzing in your mind."

Right then, a mosquito buzzed around my ear. I swatted it away with a sudden surge of anger. I wanted to hurt that stupid bug. Just like I wanted to hurt Talia. I was so sick of her—

My eyes went wide. The mosquitoes! There seemed to be one buzzing nearby every time I entertained bad thoughts. Fearmonger smiled as he watched me start to understand. "Buzz buzz buzz! And type type type." I frowned, confused. "Don't you just hate Talia?" he said, snapping his fingers. My phone buzzed in my pocket. I pulled it out and stared at the message.

> **Skeeter999:**
> Don't you just hate Talia?

I suddenly felt like I was going to throw up. Skeeter. Mosquito. How did I not see that before?

"You're...you're Skeeter999," I stammered. Fearmonger took a dramatic bow. When he stood back up, he seemed to be even bigger than he was a minute ago.

Joph was shaking in anger beside me. "I've had enough of your interference, bug," he growled. "It's time to go."

"I don't have to go anywhere, you big sack of glitter!" Fearmonger hissed. "She opened the door to her heart, and I walked right on in. You can't make me leave."

"Maybe not," Joph said, "but she can."

Joph looked at me. Fearmonger looked at me. I looked at Fearmonger. Then I looked at Joph.

"Me?" I blurted. "What can I do?"

"Nothing," sneered Fearmonger. "You can't stop me. I've infected your brother. I've infected Talia. And now I've infected you."

I was shaking. He was right. I felt hopeless, powerless. What could I do?

I heard a clang and looked down to see my golden breastplate wobbling on the ground. I watched the other pieces of armor fall off as my fear grew. As I stared at the fallen armor, Fearmonger lunged at me. I didn't even have time to scream as Joph rushed forward and slapped him away. But right before he did, I felt a poke from Fearmonger's nose, just above my heart.

"Don't you touch her!" Joph roared, and then chased after Fearmonger. Before he could clasp the bug in his hands, Fearmonger flew over top of him and buzzed in circles around the big angel. Joph grabbed his sword from his back and slashed at Fearmonger. But the demon didn't dodge this time—he caught the blade between his warty claws. Both supernatural creatures struggled, locked in battle. I stood there in shock, glued to the patch of grass I was standing on. There was a cold pain spreading from where Fearmonger poked me.

How could this ugly creature be tough enough to fight a giant angel warrior? When I had first met him, he was small and weak. He seemed to have no power except his words. Unless...unless I was the one giving him power.

Oh no.

All the terrible thoughts and doubts I'd had...all the things I'd written in that Bruise Book. Was this my fault? So many seeds in so many places, and I'd been letting them all grow. Was he feeding off my fears? Maybe I wasn't strong enough to fight this awful creature. I couldn't do this! I couldn't do this!

I touched my chest and felt something slimy. I looked down and saw...a tiny seed, sprouting through my shirt above my heart. The color drained from my face. I tried to flick the seed away, but it wouldn't budge. It was stuck to me like superglue. I scraped. I screamed. Nothing.

Fearmonger changed course and flew at me again, but Joph grabbed his feet and whipped him up and over his head, smashing him into the ground. I shielded my face as rocks and dirt went flying. All the faith and hope I had was washed away as fear flooded through my body, and I felt like I had just plunged into icy cold water. I couldn't do this! This wasn't real! None of this is real!

And when I opened my eyes again...they were both gone, and I was completely alone. No. Not alone. There was someone standing in the middle of the clearing near the playhouse, silhouetted by the setting sun. The figure took a step closer, and I could see her clearly now. Talia blocked my way. And she looked furious.

"T-Talia?" I stuttered. "What are you doing here?"

"You made me look stupid in front of everyone today," she growled. I'd seen Talia mad, but this was next level mad.

I suddenly felt like I was going to puke. "Did you come here to beat me up?"

"I came here because I found this." She held up my War Eagles keychain. Aw, boogers.

"I found this by my backyard. Did you come to my house? Did you talk to my sister?" I stood there silently, not knowing what to say. "Why can't you just mind your own business? Why can't you just leave me alone? I don't need you in my life! I don't need anyone!" Talia threw the keychain at my feet. "Don't talk to me ever again, okay?"

I said nothing.

"Yell at me back!" she ordered.

"No," I managed to squeak out.

"Stop being so perfect! Yell at me!" she screamed, and suddenly burst into tears. I stood there in in shock. I had never seen her cry. "Yell at me…" she said between sobs. "I deserve it." She sniffed hard and smeared her tears across her shirt sleeve. "I…this is stupid. I shouldn't have come here. Just…just leave me alone."

"I'm not going to leave you," I said, before I could stop myself. My heart was talking faster than my mouth now. "I know we aren't friends anymore. But I don't want to be enemies. When we were friends, I…I saw something special in you, even when no one else could. I know it's still there, because..." My words were like sand in my mouth, but something deep inside me pushed me to keep talking. "I know it's still there, because God put it there."

Talia took another step toward me, and in the dimming light I could still see her eyes flash with anger. But what really caught my eye was the monstrously huge fear seed that covered Talia's whole chest and stomach. Roots were seeping out of it and spreading over her legs, arms, and neck. And the seed was pulsing. It was disgusting.

"Stop talking about God like He's real and He cares," she said, as Fearmonger soared past my head and landed beside her, still clutching the Bruise Book. I glanced over my shoulder, but I was alone. Where was Joph? Fearmonger crouched down, put a warty arm around Talia's shoulder, and poked her in the neck with his pointy nose. Talia didn't seem to notice, her anger toward me rising. "I've had about enough of you and how perfect you always have to be!"

Fearmonger held up a rusty metal watering can and sprinkled something that did not look like water onto Talia's chest. Her fear seed pulsed, and a slight crack appeared down the middle. Talia was yelling at me now, but I couldn't even hear her. I realized that I felt sorry for Talia. Was she so controlled by fear that she didn't even know what was happening? It was like I had stepped out of that reality into another dimension, where it was just me and Fearmonger.

Fearmonger barked out a wicked laugh. "I told you, this is the end. You lose. You can't help Talia. You can't help your brother. You can't even help yourself. Look at you. No armor. No angel. No... Guy in the sky." Fearmonger pointed up, refusing to say God's name.

"You are all alone." He turned to Talia, who seemed hypnotized, and held up the Bruise Book. "Let's see what page one says, shall we?" Reading from it, he whispered into Talia's ear. "November 11. Today, Talia and I stopped being friends. I didn't do anything to her. I'm a nice person! What's her problem? Well, I will still be kind, even if she is going to be a big stupid jerk."

As Fearmonger read, Talia continued to yell. "And why do you keep trying to be nice to me? I know you think I'm just a big stupid jerk!" Fearmonger dumped the rest of the disgusting liquid from the watering can onto her, and the fear seed split in half with a large crack. Fearmonger began laughing a terrible laugh. And I watched as a creepy little root wiggled its way out of the seed, then another, and another. Suddenly disgusting black roots exploded out from Talia's chest, growing impossibly fast. They twisted and shot up all around me like a dark forest of fear roots, closing in around me, blocking out all light, reaching for me with sharp, claw-like branches.

DISCUSSION QUESTIONS

Every prayer is powerful. Do you believe that? Why or why not?

Fearmonger called Zoe "Little Failure," which is the opposite of what Joph called her (Little Warrior). Have you ever pictured yourself in your mind as the opposite of how God sees you? Joph also called Zoe these names: Little Warrior, Tiny Champion, Daughter of God, Tenderheart. Can you think of some good names that God might call you?

Fearmonger turned out to be Skeeter999 and was putting thoughts into people's heads. What do we need to do with those bad thoughts?

Chapter 14

THE COMMANDER

I was blind.

I was trapped in total darkness, surrounded by a forest of fear growing out of Talia's seed. I groped in the dark, brushing against branches that moved around wildly like angry snakes. I stepped back in disgust and fell to the ground. I clutched my chest to slow my pounding heart, but it was covered by the seed Fearmonger had placed on me. And it was growing. No, no, no. This couldn't be real. This couldn't be happening. I was standing on the path by my playhouse, just me and Talia. There were no evil fear forests, no demons...no angels? I shook my head. I had to believe angels were real. Because if angels were real, God was real. And He was my only hope right now. I realized that I was caught in a spiritual battle for Talia's heart, and I couldn't help her alone.

As I clung to that hope, a small light began to glow softly from underneath the seed on my chest, giving just enough light to see Fearmonger buzzing far above me. A branch lunged at me, trying

to grab my wrist. I yanked my arm out of its grasp. Hurting people hurt people, I remembered. Talia was letting out all her fear, all her hurt, and I was in the way of all of it. Well, I had definitely stepped into her mess. Now what?

Fearmonger laughed wickedly as he soared above my head, clutching my Bruise Book. He was still reading, spilling all my awful secret thoughts. I dodged another branch attack and cried out. "God! I know You're real! I know You care! I need help!" I gasped, frantic. "I need answers! I need to...wait."

I hadn't noticed it until right now, but amidst all the fear and craziness, there was something else I felt. This little surge of power and confidence. Almost as if someone was straightening my shoulders, helping me stand taller and feel bigger.

Joph?

I couldn't see him, but somehow I knew he was there. My nose suddenly felt warm. Did I...did I just get booped? The warmth that started at my nose was spreading through me, so I closed my eyes and took a deep breath. The light from my chest seemed to shine a bit brighter.

"Hey!" Fearmonger snarled, trying to get my attention. "Are you listening to me?"

"No," I replied calmly.

"No? What do you mean, no? What are you doing?" he yelled.

I let out a long, slow breath from my nostrils. The corners of my lips curved up slightly into a mischievous smirk. "I'm waiting."

"Waiting?" Fearmonger cackled in laughter. "For what? I've already beaten you. Things can't get any worse than this!"

"Maybe not. But they can get a whole lot better."

I stood there, silent. I ignored the fear forest around me and the cackling creep above me. My lips began to move, although no words were coming out. The world around me quieted and slowed. It was just me and the thoughts flowing around in my head. The swirling storm of cluttered thoughts parted and made way for a glowing thought, which hovered in front of my mind.

I opened my eyes. I wasn't trapped in a forest of fear. I was standing in a room of bright white, with a beautiful throne in the center. And standing in front of the throne, dressed in shining armor and a dazzling crown, was Someone I instantly recognized.

"Hello, Zoe," He said, with a voice that sounded like a hug feels. "I was hoping you'd come here."

Grayzon stood in the trees, watching his sister and Talia. As soon as she had gone out the front door, he had felt a tug in his heart, telling him to follow her. He tried to ignore the feeling, but it wouldn't go away. It was probably nothing, but...she was his sister. And Dad always said family was everything.

Peering through the branches, Grayzon tried to understand what was happening. Why was Zoe standing there looking so scared? Why was she letting Talia yell at her like that? This seemed stupid, risky, dangerous even.

But then again, that's what Zoe loved. At least, she used to, before he broke his leg. She was different now, scared to try things, worried about what could happen. He could see it in her eyes. But his sister used to love adventures, and she always wanted him to join her. Whether it was playing in waterfalls or jumping off roofs onto trampolines, she cheered him on. And to be honest, he loved it. She was a great sister. Why was he being so hard on her? She had said sorry more times than he could count. It wasn't her fault, really. He chose to jump.

Grayzon crept closer until he could hear what they were saying. Talia was yelling every mean thing she could think of, but he couldn't hear Zoe. She was moving her lips, but...oh. How could Zoe be praying while all this was happening? It was as if she was in the middle of another dangerous stunt. And just like when he was standing on the roof looking at the trampoline below him, he needed to choose if he would follow her into another risky adventure.

The faith he had ignored for so long suddenly roared to life inside him. He didn't know what Zoe was trying to do, but he could join her anyway. He could choose to jump again. Grayzon closed his eyes and began to pray for his sister.

My eyes took in all His features at once—eyes that burned brightly like a cozy campfire, strong shoulders that would be perfect for shoulder rides, a powerful frame that looked like it could carry the weight of the world—and an entirely different kind of fear swept through me. I could feel His presence, like warm sunshine on my skin. I didn't know what else to do, so I fell to my knees and bowed my face to the ground. After a few moments, I heard His footsteps get closer.

"I know this is overwhelming," He said. "But please, don't be shy. You are My child. You can talk to Me like a Father. Because I am your Heavenly Father."

I spoke softly. "Am I...in heaven? Or am I seeing this in my mind?"

"Does it matter?" He said. "The only thing you need to know is that I am here with you, right now. And I am very real."

I felt a hand grab mine, and He pulled me to my feet. He smiled, and it felt like ten thousand happy moments high-fiving my heart at the same time. I immediately yelled excitedly and jumped for joy. Eventually, I calmed down and caught my breath. He seemed to be enjoying every second of it.

"Heh. Joph was right about Your smile," I said, wiping a happy tear from my eye. "Wait, where is Joph?" I asked, looking around.

"I know that sometimes it's hard to tell, but he's still there, standing right behind you. Even when it seems like you're all alone, you're not. I've made sure of it."

"I have so many questions," I said. He laughed, and I immediately started yelling and jumping for joy again.

"I know you have questions," He said, when I finally calmed down. "And we've got your whole life to answer them. Just keep coming back here." He put His arm around me, and we started to walk. "I know sometimes it feels like you're waiting for Me to do things. But the truth is, you're not waiting for Me—I'm waiting for you."

"Waiting for me? What do you mean?"

"I have so much I want to do in your life, Zoe." When He said my name, it felt like butterflies in my stomach were tickling me from the inside out. "So many things I want to do through you. But I'll never make you do anything. I want you to want to do it."

I stopped and looked into His eyes. "I do want to! I'll do whatever You want! I guess...I just don't always know what You want, or what I should do. But at least now I know You're here with me, and You've sent angels to protect me."

"Absolutely. My angels are all around you. But do you want to know what's even cooler? I am in you." He touched me just above my heart, in the same place that Fearmonger had poked me. "Boop."

Instantly every worry and fear melted away as His love and power surged through me. I breathed in the biggest breath I'd ever taken in my life. "You just booped me."

He winked. "Where do you think Jophiel got the idea? Now... it's time to go, child."

"No!" I begged desperately. "I want to stay here with You!"

He gave me a soft smile. "I need to spend time with a little girl that I love with all My heart."

"I know You love me! That's why I want to stay!"

"I wasn't talking about you," He said.

"You weren't? Then...oh," I said, understanding. "You mean Talia."

"Yes. I love her so much. She is so special to Me."

I looked at Him and saw that He really, truly meant it. In His eyes, Talia was His perfect child. He saw her the way she was meant to be. Right then and there, I made a decision.

"If You love her, then I will too."

He nodded approvingly.

"Thank You for spending time with me," I said.

"That's funny," He replied, "I was just about to say the same thing to you." I took a deep breath and closed my eyes, ready to face whatever was waiting for me. "Wait!" He shouted. I opened my eyes, startled. Before I could ask what was happening, He scooped me up and gave me a big hug. I closed my eyes and squeezed Him back, enjoying this special moment.

I sighed dreamily. "You're the best."

DISCUSSION QUESTIONS

While the battle raged between Fearmonger and Joph, Zoe quieted herself and found herself in a conversation with God, her Heavenly Father. (God is real! Do you believe that?) Wouldn't it be super cool to have a conversation like Zoe had with God? You can!

Do you know the spirit world is very very real?

Like Grayzon, have you ever felt God tug at your heart and realized you needed to make a choice?

Chapter 15

SCREAMS AND SWORDS

When I opened my eyes, I was once again surrounded by the tangled roots of the fear seed sprouting from Talia's chest.

"What just happened?" demanded the huge monstrous form of Fearmonger, who was standing right in front of me. He still clutched my Bruise Book in his claws, but he was shaking.

"I was just spending some time with God."

Fearmonger flinched at the mention of God's name, and I thought I saw him shrink a little. "It doesn't m-m-matter!" he yelled, stuttering on the last word. "You're beaten! Your angel's left you! You have no hope!"

"My hope isn't in an angel," I said. "My hope is in the One who sent the angel."

"Stop talking about Him!" yelled Fearmonger, and he seemed to shrink a little more. "Shut up!"

"No, you shut up. You're not big and scary," I said, realizing his secret. I closed my eyes and took a breath, encouraging myself to be brave. "You feed off fear, but you're not a gigantic monster. You're a tiny little liar. And I see you for who you really are." When I opened my eyes, Fearmonger had been transformed back to the small lumpy creature he had been at the start.

"What have you done?" he screamed at me.

I stepped forward. "You don't get to scare me anymore. I'm done with the lies you've told me and Grayzon and Talia! We don't want those awful thoughts in our heads anymore! You need to leave us alone!"

"Ooh, big words!" Fearmonger spat on the ground in front of me. "What are you gonna do, attack me with your angel buddy's sword?"

"I don't need his sword." I smiled. "I have my own." I held out my hand and, with a level of authority I didn't realize I had, spoke the Bible verse Dad repeated to us all the time. "I capture every thought, and make it obey Christ." The air around me shimmered and warped as a huge golden sword materialized in my hand. I stared in awe at the sparkling Sword of the Spirit, sharp and deadly to all those who stood in the way of Truth.

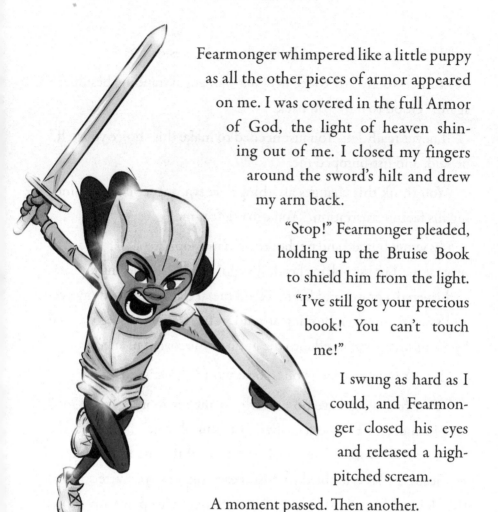

Fearmonger whimpered like a little puppy as all the other pieces of armor appeared on me. I was covered in the full Armor of God, the light of heaven shining out of me. I closed my fingers around the sword's hilt and drew my arm back.

"Stop!" Fearmonger pleaded, holding up the Bruise Book to shield him from the light. "I've still got your precious book! You can't touch me!"

I swung as hard as I could, and Fearmonger closed his eyes and released a high-pitched scream.

A moment passed. Then another.

The ugly little demon opened one clenched eye. He looked down at his body to check for holes, then looked up in surprise and stared at his hands. His wart-covered claws still grasped the Bruise Book...which was now chopped in half.

"Why..." Fearmonger sputtered. "Why did you do that?"

"Because I don't need that book anymore," I declared.

"That was awesome," said a familiar voice beside me.

I turned to my side to see my guardian angel standing beside me again. "Good to have you back."

"I never really left. You just needed to make this choice yourself," he said, and fist-bumped me.

"You think this changes anything?" Fearmonger yelled, pounding his feet in frustration. "You can't defeat me!"

His wings buzzed and he shot toward me. Joph stepped forward to protect me, but I shook my head. "I've got this," I said, closing my eyes. I whispered a prayer and heard a loud metal clang. I opened my eyes and saw Fearmonger, buzzing around in frustration, his leg trapped by a long chain anchored into the ground. He roared in anger.

"I don't need to touch you to beat you! My fear seeds—"

"Your fear seeds have no power over me anymore. I have God's love in me, and His perfect love casts out all fear." I touched the blade of the Sword of the Spirit to the seed that had sprouted on my heart, and it crumbled to dust. Fearmonger's eyes were so wide they looked like dinner plates. "And if you try to plant any more, I'll know. I've got heavenly help." I pointed my Sword at Joph, who clanged his sword against mine.

"You haven't beaten me!" Fearmonger shrieked, thrashing against his chains like a kite caught in a windstorm. "My voice is everywhere! I can stir up panic on your phone..."

I pulled out my phone and clicked a few buttons. "Skeeter999, duh-leted."

Fearmonger sputtered. "I—I can whisper in any ear!"

A mosquito buzzed by my head. Puddles popped up from the hood of my War Eagles hoodie and shot her tongue at the bug, catching it and pulling it back into her mouth.

Crunch.

I patted my frog on her head and smiled. "You were saying?"

"But, but...you're just a little kid!" Fearmonger screamed.

"No I'm not!" I screamed back, pointing my Sword of the Spirit at his ugly wart-covered face. Fearmonger flew backward, as if I'd punched him with an invisible fist. "I'm the heavily guarded treasure of heaven!"

"Oh snap!" Joph cheered.

I planted a foot in front of me and took a big breath. "GET OUT OF HERE..."

Joph began to bounce up and down, gleefully repeating, "Here it comes here it comes here it comes..."

"...IN THE NAME OF JESUS!" I screamed those words as loud as I could, and it blasted out of me like a hurricane. Beside me, I saw Joph holding his sword like a guitar, and with a swing of his mighty arm, as if striking a guitar chord, light surged forward and

consumed Fearmonger. It was as if my words released the power of heaven itself and were now blasting the enemy.

Fearmonger screamed in pain as the chain on his foot was vaporized and he was violently blasted into the sky, bits of warts and wings falling down to the crater in the ground left by the explosion of energy. I watched the little demon spin away until he was a speck in the sky.

For a long while, there was total silence.

"AND DON'T COME BACK!" Joph yelled, which made me jump in surprise. Then he burst into a fit of laughter. As Joph began dancing around, I looked again at the forest of dark roots surrounding us. My whole body was vibrating, but I couldn't tell if it was because I was so energized with God's presence or because I was so exhausted from giving everything I had. I wanted to run a marathon and take a nap at the same time.

The tangled black branches that had sprouted from Talia began to shudder, little bits of ash falling off of them. An awful squeal filled the air, causing me to cover my ears. "What's happening?" I said. Joph and I stood back to back in a protective stance, swords out and ready.

"Your prayer didn't just free you!" yelled Joph. "It loosened the hold Fearmonger had on Talia! Now she can see the truth of what was holding her, and she can break free!"

All around me, the branches were beginning to shrivel and die. And the sound…it was as if the branches were squealing in pain. But as I listened, I noticed another sound. At the center of the twisted forest of roots, Talia was screaming.

"She's in pain!" I said as I ran through the branches. I didn't even wait to see if Joph was following me. The roots weren't trying to grab me anymore—instead, they seemed to be clawing at the ground, trying to stop themselves from withering away to nothing. I slashed at a flapping branch with my Sword of the Spirit and hopped over another cluster of branches that were whipping around like snakes in a clothes dryer. I used every trick I had learned in basketball practice to dodge and weave around the branches as I got closer and closer to the heart of the roots.

I was almost there. At the center of the forest, I could see Talia struggling to her feet, holding tightly to the gnarled tree trunk coming out of her heart, as if hugging it and refusing to let go. I started to shout to Talia, but she cut me off with an even louder scream. That's when I realized she wasn't hugging the trunk—she was pulling it out. She shook and yelled as she gave the trunk one final tug, and it ripped free. The trunk crashed to the ground and exploded into ash as Talia fell to her knees.

I stood a few feet away from Talia, who was breathing heavily. I sheathed my Sword and the Armor of God faded from my view, although I knew it was still there. Talia wiped sweat off her forehead and whispered, "It wouldn't get out of my way. So I made it move."

"You sure did."

Talia finally looked up at me. "What the heck just happened?!"

Where would I even start? Well Talia, there was this seed and a mosquito demon and exploding roots and a sword and angel... Um, no. That might be a bit much. Instead, I told her the simplest truth I could think of. "I was praying for you. And God just helped your heart." I expected her to argue with me, saying prayer was stupid or that God was imaginary, but she just nodded slowly. She seemed to be in shock.

"I don't understand. I was yelling, and then you were praying, and I felt all this awfulness inside of me come rushing to the surface, and I just wanted it gone so bad..."

"And is it gone? The awfulness?" I asked hopefully.

Talia rubbed her forehead as if she had a headache. "I don't know. I can't even remember why I came here now." She looked around, noticing she was standing in the clearing. Her eyes stopped on the playhouse, and I could almost see the pain in her eyes as she remembered that night she had stormed out, declaring we would never be friends again.

In that moment, I so desperately wanted Talia to hug me and say sorry a million times and admit it was all her fault and tell me she would never be mean again as long as she lived...but she didn't do any of that. She didn't say anything at all.

Instead, I said the last thing I expected to come out of my mouth. "Talia, I'm sorry for being so mean to you. Will you forgive me?"

My greatest enemy stared at me in total confusion. "But...I'm the one who says all the mean things and embarrasses you. What have you done?"

I glanced at the mangled half of the Bruise Book, laying open on the ground between us. "I've been holding on to some pretty awful thoughts about you, and I don't want to be trapped anymore."

Talia was quiet for a few seconds, and then put her hands on her hips. "You really believe all this stuff? God, forgiveness, the whole deal?"

"Yeah. I do."

She cracked her knuckles nervously just like she always did when the teacher called on her in class. "Fine. I...forgive you."

I let out a breath. "Thanks."

"Huh, I guess Zoe the Perfect isn't so perfect after all," she said with a slight smirk.

"Nope," I said, smiling back. "And I guess Talia the Terrible isn't so terrible after all."

Talia turned to leave. I don't know what made me do it, but I did the most ridiculous thing I could have done. I stuck out my fist and said, "Wait!" Talia looked back at my fist and raised an eyebrow.

"Seriously?" she scoffed. She puffed out her chest like she always did when she wanted to act tough, but this time I could see a softness in her eyes that was trying to come out. I kept my hand out, and she sighed. "Fine. Just this once."

Bump, bump, slap, slap, slide, bump, elbows, knees, finger wiggles, bump.

"Don't ever tell anyone I did that," she said. Then she walked away without another word.

As I watched Talia disappear down the path, I heard a soft scraping coming from the playhouse. I looked just in time to see the roots of the fear seeds shriveling up, and the seed itself crumbling to dust. Joph was right. It had taken more than one simple prayer to destroy the seed. It hadn't been easy, but I finally could see hope for Talia and I, whatever that would look like. Joph appeared beside me, which startled me back to reality. I hadn't even realized he'd been gone. "Where were you just now?"

"Talking with Talia's angel."

"Talia has an angel too?!" I blurted out, and immediately felt stupid. Of course she did.

"Oh yeah, he's great," said Joph. "He's been working really hard to help her, and he's so excited for what's happening now that she's free from that seed. He told me to say thank you."

"He's thanking me?" I said in shock.

"Of course. You helped him on his mission," said Joph. I kicked a branch away and Joph frowned. "What's the matter?"

"I guess I was just hoping Talia would instantly love God like I do. We went through all this, and I don't even know if she's changed."

"It's not your job to know that. Just give her time. The Commander gave you a special mission—to be a reflection of Jesus to Talia. This was a good start. No matter what happens, stay strong and keep praying. The Commander is doing something really big in these special days, and He needs all His children to do their part."

We stood silently on the path together, watching the last rays of sunlight disappear. Birds chirped happily in the trees nearby, and Joph giggled softly. I assumed one of the birds had just told a joke. I heard a rustling behind me and turned to see all the scattered pages of my Bruise Book flapping around the clearing. Joph rested a hand on my shoulder and winked at me. He blurred out of focus, and a second later he was holding all the papers and the other half of my journal.

"Want to see something cool?" he said. I nodded, and Joph burst into flames, incinerating the pages. A second later, he was normal again. Well, as normal as a nine-foot-tall armored angel can get.

"That was amazing!" I said. Then a thought hit me. "Wait, you could do that all along? I smacked my head the whole way here in the dark, and you could have been my walking night light!" Joph frowned at me, and I grinned sheepishly. "Just kidding." I decided to change the subject. "Did that really all happen? Exploding seeds and evil branches?"

"What you saw was more of a picture of what was happening in Talia's heart. The battle you fought was real, though. Absolutely. Your whole life, He will give you chances—"

"Don't you mean missions?" I corrected.

Joph smiled. "Yes. He will give you missions to help people who are hurting, to pray for them and bring freedom from the terrible things that have planted roots in their hearts and minds. It's a big mission. Do you think you're up for it?"

I considered it, and then saluted Joph. "Absolutely. I can do anything if I place my trust in God."

"Yeah," Joph sighed dreamily. "He's the best." He saluted me back, and we turned to leave. I looked up at the spot where Fearmonger disappeared into the sky.

"Is that little creep gone for good?" I asked.

"Probably not," said Joph. "But if he comes back, he'll be smaller. And quieter. You know what to do if he tries to cause any more trouble. But keep an eye out. Fear loves to creep into your life in lots of different ways. The things you see on TV, the stories people share..."

"I'll be wise," I said, "so he can't lie to me with his proper Gandalf."

"Propaganda," Joph corrected.

"Purple gander?"

Joph just shook his head. "You'll get it. But don't worry about that right now. There are other things to focus on." Joph pointed back toward my house. Standing on the path, watching me with a look of pure shock, was my brother Grayzon.

DISCUSSION QUESTIONS

The last piece of armor Zoe received was the Sword of the Spirit, which is the Bible. What are some scriptures from the Bible you can use to fight your battles? Can you memorize some scriptures to use when you need them?

Zoe asked forgiveness from Talia, even though Talia was the one who did all the bullying. Asking for forgiveness frees you. Sometimes we have to do the apologizing, even if the other person is just as responsible for the problem. Can you think of someone you need to apologize to, even though they're the one at fault? It will make you both feel better.

Were you surprised to find out that Talia has an angel, too? We ALL have angels!

Can you think of a time you have helped someone who was hurting?

Chapter 16

GOOD NIGHT, ANGEL

"What are you doing?" I asked as I approached my brother.

"I followed you. What were you doing, Zoe?" he replied.

"Um, that depends. What exactly did you see?" I really hoped he wasn't going to say "evil trees."

Grayzon scratched his head. "I saw Talia yelling at you. And you were praying for her. Then I started praying for you, and—"

"Whoa, what?" I said with astonishment. "You were praying for me?"

"Um, yeah." Grayzon blushed. "I saw something amazing happen as you prayed for her and stood your ground against whatever was trying to control her. It was like there was this, I don't know, spiritual battle happening. Does that make sense?"

I held back a giggle. "More than you know."

Grayzon continued. "Then you ripped up a book and she started crying and you asked for forgiveness and then you guys did a dorky fist bump thing..."

"It's not dorky!" I said defensively.

"It's super dorky. But..." Grayzon paused. "But I saw what happens when someone forgives and lets go of hurt and anger. I didn't think there was any hope for you two, but...you made a way where there was no way." I smiled and Grayzon sighed. "Zoe, I know you weren't trying to get me injured on the trampoline. And I know you feel awful about what happened. I just want you to know...I forgive you. I'm learning how to be better. It seems like you are too. I don't know how to do this stuff well. But for now, here's a little taste of forgiveness."

Then my brother hugged me. After a few stunned seconds, I hugged him back. Really, really hard. And when I let go, I watched in wonder as the fear seed that had been growing on his back fell out of his shirt and dissolved into the dirt path.

"I just have one more question," he said, as we walked toward the house. "Who were you talking to just a second ago?"

I glanced at Joph, who nodded encouragingly. I grinned at my brother. "Don't freak out, okay?"

Grayzon took the news surprisingly well. I wasn't one hundred percent sure he believed I had an invisible guardian angel on a mission to protect me...but he didn't make fun of me, which was a good start. When we walked in the door, Grayzon kicked off his shoes and started up the stairs.

"Where are you going in such a hurry? I thought you beat Alien Exterminator already."

"I did. I'm going to go on the internet and research angels."

"Pfft. You don't need to do that. You can read everything you need to know in the report I'm working on for Mrs. Koopmans' class. I'm going to finish it right now."

Grayzon nodded. "Okay, I'll read it in the morning. Good night."

"Good night," I said, walking over to the Chromebook. Puddles hopped out of my hood and sat on the desk, as if supervising my homework. I added in some final notes about what I had learned today.

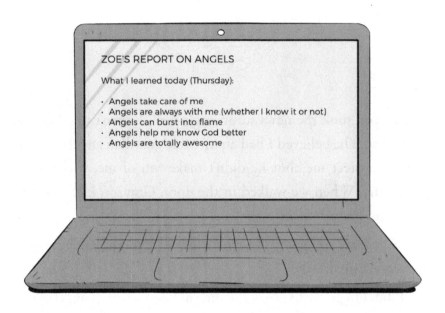

I spent the next hour typing away until I finally yawned and closed the Chromebook. Tomorrow was Friday, one week since I had been given this assignment. So much had happened in that time. I opened my message app and started a group chat with Aaliyah and Bennett.

> **WarEagle4Life:**
> Did you guys finish your reports? I just finished.
> I'm actually really excited to share about angels.
> I've definitely learned a lot this week

> **FutureMissPresident:**
> Way to go, girl, I bet you crushed it! Bennett
> can make fun of me all he wants for picking
> Bigfoot, but he won't be laughing when I
> get a higher grade than him

> **BenBen1010:**
> way to go Zoe my report is gonna be way better than Aaliyahs cuz Pegasus is awesome and he can fly super fast

> **WarEagle4Life:**
> I bet he couldn't outrun an angel though lol

> **BenBen1010:**
> probably not but he would beat bigfoot for sure

> **FutureMissPresident:**
> None of that will matter when I destroy you with my amazing grade. I'm going to

I rolled my eyes and closed the app without reading the rest. Those two never stopped. I had just finished getting ready for bed when Mom came into my room to tuck me in.

"Zoe, your brother mentioned that your journal got wrecked tonight."

"Oh, um, yeah."

"Well then, here you go." She held up a brown leather journal with a gold strap and the words Beauty Book written on the front. It was identical to my old one.

I gasped. "Mom, how..."

"Oh, I've had it sitting in a drawer for years," she said. "You know me—I always buy two of everything."

I hugged her and gently placed the book in my desk drawer. Another chance at a fresh start. This time, I was going to use my journaling powers for good instead of for evil. Dad joined us and they both prayed for me. I smiled, knowing that now all three of my family members had prayed for me today. Puddles croaked good-night from her tank as they shut the door behind them.

Joph appeared beside me. "What a day, huh?"

"Yeah. Thank you for everything, Joph. Thanks for letting me meet you."

"It was my greatest honor, Little Warrior," Joph said softly. "And just think about how blessed all those kids out there are who've never seen an angel, but still confidently believe that they are being protected and strengthened. That's pretty awesome."

"So awesome," I said. "Joph...will I ever see you again?"

He shrugged. "Maybe. Maybe not. That's up to The Commander. But don't spend your days looking for me. Look for The Commander. He shows Himself to you the most realest way possible."

We both sighed dreamily. "He's the best," we said at the same time.

Joph chuckled. "Enough questions. It's time to sleep."

I yawned a deep, long yawn. "Feel free to have some Fruitee-Os while you stand guard," I said. "They're on the table."

"Sweet!" Joph said. "I bet they taste better in a bowl than they do dripping down my armor."

"You're not going to let me forget that, are you?"

"Nope."

I looked into Joph's golden eyes and smiled. "God sure must love me if He sent me someone like you." Joph smiled and gave me a tiny salute. As he turned to go, I grabbed his pinky. "Joph? One more thing," I whispered.

He leaned in close. "Yes?"

I tapped him on the nose. "Boop." Joph blinked in surprise, and I gave him a lazy grin. "Told you I'd get you back."

Little kid and holy being both chuckled softly. Joph stood at attention and waited until my rhythmic breathing was the only sound in the room. The last thing I saw as my eyes drooped closed was Joph silently tiptoeing down the stairs toward the Fruitee-Os.

DISCUSSION QUESTIONS

What did you think about angels before you read this book? What do you think about them now?

Zoe got rid of her Bruise Book and has a Beauty Book again. What would the title of your life journal be?

Which character in this story did you identify with the most? Do you need to make a change in your life? You can talk to God right now.

?

EPILOGUE

I woke up Friday morning feeling like a brand-new person. I had dreamed a beautiful dream about white light, a beautiful throne, and a smiling Commander surrounded by His army of angels. Dad made waffles for the second morning in a row, which never happens. It was like he somehow knew I had something to celebrate. Grayzon read my report while we ate breakfast and told me I did a really great job. We even made plans to go for a bike ride together in the evening.

When I got to school, I proudly plopped my report down onto Mrs. Koopmans' desk and strutted toward my desk, looking hopefully at Talia. I wondered if Talia would jump up on her desk and declare God was the best, or that she vowed never to hurt anyone again with her words, or that she and I were going to be besties again...but she didn't do any of that. She didn't say anything at all. My permanent morning smile faded slightly as Talia spent the whole class avoiding my eyes. I wanted to say something, but it didn't feel like the right thing to do.

Bennett and Aaliyah were still arguing over whose report Mrs. Koopmans loved more as we flooded out of the classroom for lunchtime. As I began to push through the crowded hallway, I felt a tug on my backpack. I turned and Talia bumped her way past me. It was really loud in the hallway, but I could have sworn I heard her mumble, "Sorry."

I grabbed my lunch and was shoving my backpack into my locker when I noticed something sticking out of one of the pouches. I pulled it out and stared in disbelief. It was a watch. A pink watch with the "Dream Defenders" logo. It didn't look as sparkly as it had when Talia took it two years ago, but it was definitely the same watch. I grinned the biggest grin a grinning person could grin. Yeah, there was still hope for Talia, for me, for all of us. God was making ways where there were no ways, and I was excited to be part of His Big Story. I grabbed Karissa's watch and ran to join my friends.

ZOE'S REPORT ON ANGELS

Everyone has heard about angels, but not everyone understands what they really are. In my experience, I found some surprising facts about angels.

Angels are holy beings and soldiers in God's heavenly army. Their mission is to help us with our mission—to lead us and protect us and fight for us.

Some characteristics about angels are that they are patient, caring, mysterious, and joyful. They are free to make their own choices, can look like anyone, speak only truth, and keep areas safe from evil intruders.

I think angels are lucky because they get to be in God's presence and bring that presence with them wherever they go. They are always with us (whether we know it or not), and there are so many of them!

But more than anything else, the one thing I know for sure is this: angels are real. And that brings me comfort, because it means my God is real, my God cares about me, and He sends protection to help me through my whole life. And that makes me feel pretty special.

Below are verses from the Bible, which have helped me in my research. Thank you for reading.

Psalm 91:11-13 TPT
God sends angels with special orders to protect you wherever you go, defending you from all harm. If you walk into a trap, they'll be there for you and keep you from stumbling. You'll even walk unharmed among the fiercest powers of darkness, trampling every one of them beneath your feet!

Matthew 18:10 ICB
Don't think these little children are worth nothing. I tell you that they have angels in heaven who are always with my Father in heaven.

Ephesians 6:12 ICB
We are fighting against the rulers and authorities and the powers of this world's darkness. We are fighting against the spiritual powers of evil in the heavenly world.

Hebrews 1:14 ICB
All the angels are spirits who serve God and are sent to help those who will receive salvation.

Hebrews 13:2 TPT
And show hospitality to strangers, for they may be angels from God showing up as your guests.

TALK ABOUT IT

This is a true story.

Okay, angels might not be orange giants, and there aren't fear seeds that will burst from your chest...but there really are angels and demons, spiritual battles for your soul, spiritual armor, and a God who loves you. This book probably brought up questions, and that's a good thing. Here are twenty questions for you to think and pray about, or for you to discuss with an adult like your parent or church leader.

Have you ever experienced a time when you knew God and His angels had protected you?

How do you think you would react if you saw an angel, and why?

If you could ask an angel (or better yet, God) twenty questions, what would you ask?

Fearmonger was sneaky with his lies. Where have you allowed fear to grow in your life?

If you've ever felt embarrassed about something you did and kept it a secret, why do you think God wants to help you deal with it and tell the truth even through it's scary?

Like Zoe and her Bruise Book, are you holding on to things you need to let go of, such as words you've said or thoughts you have that are hurtful toward others?

Maybe Holy Spirit is reminding you of something that you need to apologize for (or confess). The Bible says in 1 John 1:9, "If we confess our sins, he is faithful and just and will forgive us our sins and purify us from all unrighteousness." That means He will disintegrate the fear seeds so that your conscience is clear! No more fear! You can give it a try right now.

Have you ever had people make fun of you for being a Christian, going to church, or believing in God? How did it feel? How did you react, or how do you think you would react?

What does forgiveness mean, and why is it so important?

Is there someone in your life who is mean to you? Ask God to help you see them the way He does and to help you see the fear that might be attached to them so you can pray for them.

Do you think God can give you an important picture for you or for someone else? Has He ever given you a picture or spoken to your heart? You can get quiet and wait on God right now and ask Him to direct your thoughts, just like Zoe did.

What does it mean to "capture every thought and make it obey Christ"? What would that look like in your everyday life?

How do you actually put on the Armor of God? How would you recognize you have it?

Would you like to have an experience like Zoe? Why or why not? Would you like to have power over fear in your life and help other people get free from fear too?

Pray and ask God to make Himself real to you, to make the Bible make sense to you, and to show you how to put it into practice in your everyday life with your family, friends, and even people you have a hard time loving.

ACKNOWLEDGMENTS

It takes a village to raise a child, they say. It apparently also takes a village to see a book come to life. So for all my family, friends, inspirations, and people who make books a reality... thank you.

To my wife, Joy, who knows my love language is words of encouragement and told me countless times how proud she was of me: you were the fuel that kept me going. Thank you for all the nights you lovingly slept on the couch beside me while I typed words and drew pictures til the wee hours of the morning.

To my kids, Zoe, Micah and Xander: thank you for letting me bounce ideas off you. You helped me design the cover, pick the title, shape the story, and so much more. I wrote this for you. (And thank you, daughter, for giving me permission to name the main character after you.)

Thank you to my father-in-law, Brian, who taught me that prayer has the power to break strongholds. And thank you to my "mother-in-love," Connie, who told me with tears in her eyes how much this story meant to her and how badly she wants everyone to read it. That fueled a boldness inside me that made me truly believe in this book and my abilities.

To my pastors, Mike and Monica Prescott: you trusted me (even when you shouldn't have) and pushed me to do things I didn't think I could do. Someone once asked me, "What's the secret to writing a kids book?" My answer was, "Serve faithfully in your church for twenty years and let God develop you in seemingly unrelated areas (such as writing sermons, directing dinner theatres, making random youth videos, and teaching kids). Then one day it will all come together, and you'll have everything you need to dive in." Simple, right?

To Pastor Tim Sheets: thank you for the opportunity to take the truths you laid out in "Angel Armies" and find a way to unpack them for the next generation. It was so empowering to have a strong foundation from which to build on.

This book would have been a hot mess without the help of my Critique Group. Thanks, mom, for proofreading. You are the queen of grammar, and you help me type words good. Janelle Hill: thank you for blunt and genuine feedback. Considering you read over 100 fiction books a year, the fact that you truly loved this story right from the first draft is high praise indeed. Allise Bishop: your big, bold suggestions reshaped this story into something a million times better. You pretty much rewrote the entire ending for me. JoyDawn Corbeil: you have always been one of my biggest fans (well, since we became adults—we were pretty brutal to each other growing up).

Thank you for sharing your wisdom and insights. And thank you to my nephew Kaisaac, who helped keep my voice to kids accurate and true. Amy Ball: thank you for the great discussion questions! You know just what to say to get kids thinking and engaging with Jesus. Monica Prescott: thanks for making sure my theology was sound. And thanks to Jesse Hill, Samara Prescott and Amy Ewasiuk, who also read the initial draft and offered insightful tweaks and suggestions.

A huge shout out to Robynn Lang for lending me your graphic design skills. The moment I saw the finished cover was the moment I realized, "Holy cow, this is a real book."

To all my City Life Kids, I love you and am so grateful I get to play a part in your journey with Jesus. And thank you to all my friends and church family who cheered me on as I stretched my wings and learned to fly.

To the fine folks at Destiny Image, including Christian Rafetto and John Martin: I've never seen your faces but I'm grateful for all the grace and patience you gave this brand-new author. Don Nori, thank you for believing in me and pouring into me. I'm baffled at the favor God's given me through you.

This book is dedicated to Dian Layton, who inspired me to find creative ways to point children to Jesus. As she always said, "I'd rather build kids than renovate adults."

And finally, to Jesus: the only foundation to build a life on. You have truly made all things new, and I hope and pray that this story helps Your light shine through the cracks of this world and expose people to Your New Creation Reality.

ABOUT THE AUTHOR

JD Hornbacher lives in Alberta, Canada with his wife and three kids. He is a family pastor and a media producer, and he is obsessed with Jesus, family, church, and comic books. JD's secret is that he would much rather hang out with kids than with adults, because kids are way more interesting and they appreciate his random stories.

Keep in touch with JD:

Facebook: facebook.com/jdhornbacher
Instagram: instagram.com/jdhornbacher